I0802767

PRAISE FOR

Sipsworth

"In its quiet, loving way, *Sipsworth* feels as rare and special as a friend."
—*Minneapolis Star Tribune*

"Enchanting . . . fresh and often funny, thanks to the author's artful prose."
—*Publishers Weekly* (starred review)

"Charming . . . generous . . . vibrant . . . reveal[s] something profound about the human need for connection."
—*Foreword Reviews* (starred review)

"*Sipsworth* is a love story about a woman and a mouse. Reason suggests that such a relationship couldn't possibly work, and yet I found myself pulling for this unlikely duo on every page. Simon Van Booy's characters are loaded with charm, resilience, and the deep desire for connection that all mammals share. I loved it."
—ANN PATCHETT, author of *Tom Lake*

"Whimsical, beautifully detailed, and filled with heart, *Sipsworth* is a slim, sparkling jewel of a novel."
—CHRISTINA BAKER KLINE, #1 *New York Times* bestselling author of *Orphan Train*

"Through tears, laughter, joy, and pain, I just couldn't stop reading this novel about friendship and second chances. *Sipsworth* is a marvel—storytelling at its absolute finest."
—MARC LEVY, author of *All Those Things We Never Said*

PRAISE FOR

The Presence of Absence

"Tantalizing . . . some of the most beautiful prose of Van Booy's oeuvre . . . *The Presence of Absence* runs blood-rich with declarations that make you inhale sharply."
—*Washington Post*

"Van Booy electrifyingly combines story with parable. *The Presence of Absence* boggles and reverberates: wise, witty, and always breathtakingly beautiful."
—*San Francisco Chronicle*, Best Fiction of 2022

"With its elegant passages on love and the fallibility of memory . . . this indelible portrait of transience, sorrow, and hope will move readers."
—*Shelf Awareness*

"Formally playful and fable-esque . . . If you don't just like reading, but reading about reading, then this is the book for you."
—*Minneapolis Star Tribune*

"Rich in setting and emotion. As ever with Van Booy, the reader is in good hands."
—*Publishers Weekly*

"A tour de force . . . A mind-bending, affecting story that breaks the heart open with startling clarity."
—*New York Journal of Books*

"*The Presence of Absence* amazed me. It's a moving, brilliant book."
—ANN BEATTIE, author of *Onlookers*

"*The Presence of Absence* is impossible to resist. Consistently insightful, symphonic in the music of its thought."
—ILYA KAMINSKY, author of *Deaf Republic*

ALSO BY SIMON VAN BOOY

FICTION

The Secret Lives of People in Love: Stories
Love Begins in Winter: Stories
Everything Beautiful Began After
The Illusion of Separateness
Tales of Accidental Genius: Stories
Father's Day
The Sadness of Beautiful Things: Stories
Night Came with Many Stars
The Presence of Absence

NONFICTION

Why We Need Love
Why Our Decisions Don't Matter
Why We Fight

CHILDREN'S FICTION

Gertie Milk & the Keeper of Lost Things
Gertie Milk & the Great Keeper Rescue

SIPSWORTH

Sipsworth

A NOVEL

SIMON VAN BOOY

GODINE

:: BOSTON ::

Published in 2024 by
GODINE
Boston, Massachusetts

LIBRARY OF CONGRESS CATALOGING-IN-PUBLICATION DATA
Names: Van Booy, Simon, author.
Title: Sipsworth : a novel / Simon Van Booy.
Description: Boston : Godine, 2024.
Identifiers: LCCN 2023002229 (print) | LCCN 2023002230 (ebook) | ISBN 9781567927948 (hardcover) | ISBN 9781567927955 (ebook)
Subjects: LCGFT: Novels.
Classification: LCC PR6122.A36 A73 2023 (print) | LCC PR6122.A36 (ebook) | DDC 823/.92--dc23/eng/20230123
LC record available at https://lccn.loc.gov/2023002229
LC ebook record available at https://lccn.loc.gov/2023002230

ISBN 978-1-56792-875-4 (paperback)

First Paperback Printing, 2026
Printed in the United States of America

For Joshua and his father, Dale.

SIPSWORTH

OVERTURE

HELEN CARTWRIGHT WAS old with her life broken in ways she could not have foreseen.

Walking helped, and she tried to go out every day, even when it poured. But life for her was finished. She knew that and had accepted it. Each day was an impersonation of the one before with only a slight shuffle—as though even for death there is a queue.

Not a single person who glimpsed her bony figure flapping down Westminster Crescent could say they knew her. She was simply part of a background against which their own lives rolled unceasingly on. In truth, Helen Cartwright was native to the place—born in the old Park hospital while her father fought at sea. The hospital was long gone, but the brick cottage where Helen had grown up was still there. Now and again she walked that way into town. The front garden had been paved over, but cracks in the cement sometimes bled flowers she could name, as though just below the surface of this world are the ones we remember, still going on.

Her home now was a detached pensioner's cottage with a mustard door. She had purchased it through the internet after living abroad for sixty years.

A lot can happen in six decades. A place can change. But she hadn't changed.

Helen realised that the moment she had gotten out of the airport taxi and stood before the new house on Westminster Crescent. The home she had given up on the other side of the world would have other people by now. She imagined them unrolling leaves of newspaper to reveal objects that were important or fragile, but in truth were just links in a chain that led you back to the beginning.

No, she hadn't changed at all.

She simply knew more because of all the things she had been through. And contrary to the fairy tales told to her at bedtime as a child, anything of value she had returned home with was invisible to anyone but herself.

After the taxi chugged back to Heathrow, Helen had gone inside and dropped her luggage at the foot of the stairs. Like all houses, this place had its own smell that would disappear once she was used to it. On the hall floor beside her feet were letters addressed to someone she didn't know. She wondered about the people who had been here before. Tried to imagine their lives but kept returning to the husband and son, now far beyond her reach.

Still wearing her coat with the scent of aircraft cabin and coins forever loose in the seam, Helen walked through the kitchen and stood in the empty living room.

Stared out the front window.

A hundred times as a girl, she must have run, skipped, or ridden her clanking bike past this house. A hundred times as a girl, without ever thinking it a place she would return one day, to close her life in a perfect circle.

On her eightieth birthday, Helen spent the day moving things in the kitchen cupboard. Wiping down shelves. Vacuuming the stairs. Turning from any face that appeared in the dust or the darkness between cans.

Three years pass with nothing to fill their pockets.

Then early one morning, something happens.

FRIDAY

1.

IT IS PAST midnight, but still so dark, day cannot yet be separated from night. Helen Cartwright is standing at the bedroom window in her nightdress. Has nudged the curtain just enough to see a world emptied by the smallness of the hour. Unable to sleep, she is about to go downstairs and put the television on when something moves. She bends to the cold glass but loses the street in a sudden flower of breath. It clears to reveal a neighbour in robe and slippers, laden with black bags for the early-morning waste collection. Helen watches him drop his load then return to the house. Instead of locking his side gate, he props it open with a brick, then wobbles out with a large box, which he sets down on the nest of plastic bags with great care.

Over the past several months, Helen has become curious about what people throw away. Several times she has even gone out to inspect the mounds of bags for an interesting bulge—some object mistakenly tossed before its time. A hollow clunk is usually an item of wood; a delicate rattle means porcelain. Anything that sloshes is to be avoided.

And so after the neighbour has latched the side gate and locked his door, Helen steps into her tartan slippers and goes downstairs. Ensuring there is no one outside, she pulls on her coat and drops into the stomach of night. It must have been raining, for the street is like soft, damp ribbon. Helen doesn't mess with any bags. She goes straight to the large box her neighbour had been carrying, which isn't a box at all. It is a glass fish tank full of rubbish. Nothing special—except for what lies on top. A child's toy Helen has seen before—a prop from the life she has outlived, some piece of her memory that has somehow broken off and found its way back into her shaking hands.

The shape and feeling of the toy make Helen wonder if she is, in fact, upstairs in her bed sleeping soundly—and that moments later will open both eyes to the milky stillness of her room. She lets her gaze travel from the discarded object down the long row of houses on Westminster Crescent, as though a light, or a door, or the neighbour's cat might appear and break the skin of dreaming.

But nothing moves.

No one comes.

The gowned women and pajamered men of the street are the ones doused in slumber, not her. She alone brings consciousness to the moment.

Helen turns the item over. A plastic deep sea diver. Touches the air tank and flippers. Behind the diving mask two painted eyes seem to recognize her. She had bought the very same thing for her son's thirteenth birthday. Then it had been part of a set. She wonders what could be in all the small cardboard boxes underneath. Perhaps this one is part of a set, too, and the pieces will appear, one by one, as if gathered in by the long whiskers of grief.

Without thinking, she bends, heaves up the fish tank with its toy diver and dirty cardboard boxes. It's heavier than Helen has imagined, and though it isn't far to the house, halfway back, a seam of cloud opens. Everything in the aquarium is soon soaked. Water snakes down Helen's cheeks. Her head is vibrating with cold, and her hair feels sticky. There really isn't far to go—another fifteen metres—but the pooling drops increase her burden. And despite sinewy arms now swaying with strain, Helen is determined not to put the thing down. Inside, she can go through the contents and decide what to do. Memory has never come to her like this in the physical world. It has always been something weightless—strong enough to blow the day off course, but not something she can reach for and hold on to.

The weight of the fish tank with everything in it is not unlike the weight of a large child, and so she keeps on, powered by coals of instinct.

Getting the tank through the door is not easy and requires tilting. Fibres in her arms and neck writhe, and she waits for a ripping pain in her chest—but somehow there is strength left for this final test. Once in, she stumbles to the sitting room and drops the tank onto the coffee table with a thump.

After rubbing a tissue under her nose in the downstairs loo, Helen carries herself upstairs and sheds her sopping clothes. Draws a bath with a capful of eucalyptus. Lowers her shivering body into the melting water.

In warm, wet stillness she ponders the deep sea diver she can now feel holding her entire life in place like an anchor dropped years ago and then forgotten. But for what purpose is she being held at the edge? Everyone she has ever loved or wanted to love is gone, and behind a veil of fear she wishes to be where they are.

Now there is an object downstairs trying to drag her back in—a child's toy that belongs to her memory as much as it belongs to the past of another.

This sort of thing was supposed to be over for her. There is nothing in the house even to look at. No birthday cards, no letters. Even photo albums were discarded for her big move three years before. She burned them, actually. In the driveway under the terrace. She had to. Even the one of a trip to New Zealand when David was nine and they'd sat as a family with ice creams on a low wall watching small boats make for the open sea, like children leaving home.

Helen can feel steam on her face like a pair of hands. Lets her head sink back into a rolled towel. Closes her eyes against the empty rooms of her home.

Without her, it could have been anybody's house.

There had been some furniture when she arrived. A bed frame, a chest of drawers, and a modern hall table with brass legs. Curtains and carpets were also in place. The rest of her things she purchased from a catalogue. Helen had watched as two men and a woman carried in the bundles, which then had to be unwrapped and put together. She had given the workers tea and a plate of biscuits, but sat most of the time upstairs so they could talk freely and work without feeling watched. In the early evening two of them carried out the discarded packaging. The other had started the lorry and was sitting in it. On the doorstep, Helen offered something extra, in case they wanted a hot meal. There were many pubs in the town, and in the early hours of Saturday and Sunday morning, if Helen opened a window, she could hear singing or distant laughter like ripples on the surface of night.

When she was a girl, many people worked in the factories. There was one not far from her house on the other side of a canal. During her first year living on Westminster Crescent, Helen would listen for the noon whistle. But during the six decades of her absence the place had been rased and the whistle hauled off in a pile of broken brick.

It wasn't easy coming back after so long. Everything had been going on without her as if she'd never existed. The outdoor market where her mother liked to chat with the fishmonger was now a place for cars. And where the stall had been stood a tall machine that took coins for parking. The shop near the school that stayed open late for people coming home from the factory was still there. But it looked and smelled different. The burgundy awning that flapped in winter had been replaced with a white plastic sign lit up from within. And there were several tills, not just the one that stood guard before a wall of gumdrops, licorice, and sherbet.

Returning after sixty years, Helen had felt her particular circumstances special: just as she had once been singled out for happiness, she was now an object of despair. But then after so many consecutive months alone, she came to the realisation that such feelings were simply the conditions of old age and largely the same for everybody. Truly, there was no escape. Those who in life had held back in matters of love would end in bitterness. While the people like her, who had filled the corners of each day, found themselves marooned on a scatter of memories. Either way, for her as for others, a great storm was approaching. She could sense it swollen on the horizon, ready to burst. It would come and wash away even the most ordinary things, leaving no trace of what she felt had been hers.

2.

HELEN OPENS HER eyes. The bathwater has cooled. She moves her arms and legs then looks into the hall. The carpet is thin. Its once rich blue now the blue of early morning. The bathroom door, she keeps open—even when perched on the toilet wiping herself—because she *listens* to the house. There is nothing to hear, of course, but the emptiness reassures her; thoughts can wander, unfurl without touching. Helen lifts her body from the tepid water and dries herself with a towel. Dawn has come and morning's pale cheek is flat upon the world.

The fish tank is downstairs, dirty and dripping.

Helen dresses and brushes her hair. She gave up long ago on jewellery, even her wedding ring. That was the hardest. But Len had gone and would not be coming back. She had also rejected traditional ladies' slippers in favor of the more rugged tartan variety with elasticated backs and rubber bottoms. She felt ready to go, of course—had been for a while—but if she tumbled down the stairs and was unable to move, no one would find her for perhaps a year and this was somehow undesirable. Helen didn't know why, exactly, but as a child she had fallen into a disused well where she was trapped for two days.

Downstairs, Helen makes tea and flicks on the hall radio. A young man reads the morning news. When he comes to the weather, scattered showers are expected and will be general across low-lying areas. Nothing new there. But his voice fills the house as though it were his home, too.

I heard it rains day and night back in England.

This was one of the first things Leonard ever said to her. A question in the form of a statement.

They were dancing.

The year was 1960.

She had bought new shoes from Gulliver's for the dance. Kitten heels with a buckle on each toe. But no one noticed the buckles, or how they caught tiny snatches of life as she moved. Helen had met Len on a Number 7 bus the week before. This was their first proper night out.

"You should stay in Oz, love . . ."

Young Helen in new shoes kept dancing.

"Why is that, Len? Because it's sunny all the time?"

They had given their bodies to the music, but were looking at each other from worlds animated with more desire than experience.

"Not just the weather, Helen. I reckon you could have a life here if you wanted it. Go to college. Do something you enjoy. Maybe even settle down eventually with a nice fella called Len."

That was probably the moment, she thinks. Not later on the boardwalk with *I love you,* or later still in the wooden church when he said, *I do . . .* but there, then, that smoky dance hall with free lemonade and shabby curtains, tangled up in the music of childhood's end.

The memory was so intact, Helen could have looked down and fingered a button on his shirt.

She leaves the radio playing. Carries her mug to the sitting room. It is an English opera she saw once, long ago. She stands over the coffee table, slurping hot liquid with the faint but impassioned voice of Dido lamenting from the hall table. The fish tank looks bigger now that it's inside. Helen marvels at how she'd been able to carry it. Len would have clapped. But then an irritating thought alerts her to the possibility that other treasures in the bags have been missed.

Should she go back out?

The rain has stopped but is supposed to start again. And there will be people with dogs. Children mincing on their way to school.

No. That part of the day has closed to her for good. If she did go out, it had to be as a shopper or an old woman, not a scavenger rooting in rubbish.

Helen decides to spread the excitement of her find over the coming weekend while most people are glued to the television, or looping bright shops for things to buy and bring home. On Saturday morning, she will fish out every box, open it, examine the contents one by one, then carefully wash each item before setting it aside for more detailed examination on the Sunday—while something bakes in the oven. Helen has several pairs of tights that have recently fallen from grace on account of holiness at the big toe, so there will be no shortage of cleaning materials.

She returns to the kitchen with strange energy. Fills the kettle for another round of tea. When it's ready, Helen takes down the biscuit tin and carries a few brittle discs into the sitting room along with her steaming mug. Just looking at the deep sea diver atop his aquarium is enough for today, she thinks; the important thing is to have a plan and not rush.

With the biscuits gone and the sugary tea half drunk, Helen pulls her feet up onto the sofa and lets her head sink into a pillow. She stares at the fish tank before her. Below the plastic deep sea diver and under the cardboard boxes are coloured plastic objects in shapes she doesn't understand. Helen tries to imagine the last person to have touched these things. Where are those hands now and what are they doing?

As so often happens, her last thought before dozing off takes on new life as a dream: She is standing next to her son, David. They are out on the second-floor terrace. It is bright and very hot. Their clothes are many colours and large birds squabble in treetops behind the house. No one ever mentions the birds; it is just a sound they were used to. In the yard, the uncut lawn is dark and silky, a shade of shade. Len is wearing sunglasses she has chosen for him from a display at the pharmacy. The terrace wrapped around their entire house and could be accessed from every room except the toilet. Helen is about thirty-eight and standing barefoot. Her feet are small and soft on the tiles. Their son is about to open a present. He knows what it is because they had all tramped down to the pet shop a week before to help him pick everything out and to pay for it. But they'd wrapped it anyway because that's what you do with children. There is a cake somewhere. Helen doesn't see it in the dream, but knows it is just inside the screen door on a counter. After all these years. Everything that has happened. To think there is a place where your child's birthday cake still waits to be eaten.

3.

Helen sleeps right into the afternoon. As promised, the showers have been steady. The world outside is soft and dripping. The radio is still on and piano music tinkles through the house like another sort of rain.

Her tea mug is cold to the touch; that's how she judges the length of each snooze. Sometimes ten minutes feel like hours. But she'd know because the mug would still be slightly warm.

A few months ago, one of Helen's naps carried her right through the afternoon onto night's wing. She had woken in the sober presence of BBC's News at Ten. What a nuisance. Too late for supper and wide awake—she had been forced to watch television until another swell of tiredness carried her upstairs. There was a time, she remembers, when broadcasting ceased at a certain hour. People in the studio went home to crisp envelopes of bed. Now the television went all night. An endless loop of voices. Even if there was no one in the studio or watching at home, it kept on, seeking to fill the emptiness but only intensifying it.

As she lies there on the couch, watching her dream recede, Helen feels foolish for having carried into her home what is so obviously rubbish. Here is a dirty great fish tank, probably cracked somewhere under the boxes, which are likely full of dull, unwashed parts from a machine that could never be put back together.

But the deep sea diver . . . that surely *is* something.

Helen sits up and studies the thing. Nothing so personal has ever come back to her in such a way. She wonders if this being the town of her birth has anything to do with it. Perhaps more remnants of her life will soon be washing in?

For the rest of the afternoon she rearranges items in the refrigerator by colour, then watches the children's programmes that begin at four and end at five-thirty with a soap opera.

Following the contrived drama of each channel's six o'clock news, it is time for a game show. Then comedy or drama. Sometimes there are programmes with a studio audience. These are fine. If you laugh naturally with the others, it's a bit like you're there with them—caught in the same net.

At dusk, Helen stares out into the back garden. Mostly overgrown now, but quite pretty in late summer when the wind turns things over. The front lawn was paved long ago, and so spares her concerned or reproachful glances from anyone passing on foot.

Friday night dinner is usually a frozen pie cooked in the oven. The label says two servings but it's really only big enough for one and a half people. Helen considers boiling a potato to go with it, but the peeler isn't in its usual spot, and by the time she's found it, the pie is cooked through.

At the close of the nine o'clock news it's time for bed.

But going up the stairs Helen pauses midstep like a wind-up toy at the end of its run. Should she take another bath? Usually, if this desire presents itself, she will go back down and stand outside the French door for twenty minutes to freeze herself.

But it's late and it feels late.

The lights are already off downstairs and she has a job tomorrow unpacking the fish tank. If she can get her head down, it will feel like moments before she is up with tea and toast, cutting tights for the adventure ahead.

Helen continues the ascent, the sound of her feet on each stair like grunting. Without turning on a light, she locates her nightgown, then slides under the cool, musty sheets. She usually sleeps on her side, but when she is very tired, Helen sleeps on her back.

In the middle of the night, her eyes open.

Helen doesn't know why she is awake, so floats there in the steady swell of breath. Perhaps this is it. The finale. But then she hears something downstairs.

She listens again.

Very faint, but definitely there.

She keeps her body still, the way her son, David, pretended to be asleep when she arrived home from a late shift at work. Light would spill upon the cushion of his face through the open door. The boy's eyes were closed but he knew his mother was there.

This isn't a loud noise, but an insistent one.

Something is happening downstairs in her house on Westminster Crescent that hasn't happened before. A person breaking in? She knows there are burglaries in the town because it's in the local paper. But what does she have to steal? This is a place where everything of value has already been taken.

Helen peels back the covers and creeps toward the open bedroom door. It feels good to move and shake fear to the extremities. It is obvious to her now the sound is being made intentionally and there is some intelligence behind it. It isn't branches lashing the French door, or some loose chain of water from a tap in the downstairs loo. This is knocking—an impossibly light tapping like somebody small or timid is outside and wants to come in.

SATURDAY

4.

When Helen opens her eyes a few hours later, the drama of last night returns in pieces until fully intact. She had stood, listening at the bedroom door until both legs ached and she had to lie down again. In the daze of restless sleep, she convinced herself it was something insignificant she hadn't thought of: crumpled paper in the bin unballing . . . a rogue pipe knocking in the wall . . .

The idea of it being a ghost was impossible. She had given up on them long ago.

Helen ties her dressing gown and pulls on her tartan slippers. Once downstairs she searches the house for any sign of the extraordinary. But things are exactly the way they were left. Not a single object in the house exists outside of where memory has placed it.

She switches on the radio and feeds the toaster.

Fills the kettle.

Chooses a knife, which she sets between the plate and butter dish.

It is Saturday morning. Children belt past her front window on bikes and scooters. Beds are left unmade. Car doors close as families go out shopping.

While the bread is cooking, Helen peeks into the sitting room just to check the fish tank. Shuffles to the French door. Pushes back the curtain. The handle has been loose since she moved in. Helen examines it for any sign of meddling. But even the back garden thrumming with insects is undisturbed in its wildness.

After dressing properly upstairs, she's back down for the news and weather. Tights are scissored into squares, which Helen takes into the sitting room. Instead of carrying the boxes she unpacked to the sink, she fills a plastic bowl with warm, soapy water, and sets it down on the coffee table next to the fish tank. That way she can also take breaks to watch television.

She cuts, then spreads a plastic shopping bag between the fish tank and the washing bowl for each item removed from its box.

Helen's first task is to submerge the deep sea diver in suds and begin washing. Her gloves squeak over the plastic, and soap bubbles make everything glisten. It really is the same toy that brought so much happiness to David when tropical fish were his chief preoccupation. For some reason this makes her think of his shaggy hair. It annoyed him, of course, the way she brushed it with her hand, but she was his mother.

When the toy is clean and dry, Helen needs a break and makes tea. *No reason to rush things*, she reminds herself. The plastic diver has stirred up so much sediment already, it's only natural to let things settle before starting on the boxes.

After two cups of tea and a digestive biscuit, Helen sits down. Exhales. Takes a deep breath in. But her excitement dissipates as she moves the first box from the tank to the carrier bag. It is empty. Same for the second, third, fourth, fifth, and sixth boxes, which she opens just to be sure. She sits there mired in disappointment.

All she has left now are the colourful plastic things at the bottom of the tank, and one large dirty box still soggy from the downpour. As washing continues, Helen realises the plastic things must be from a play-set. One is in the shape of a castle with four turrets. Another is just a short tube. She sets both on the plastic bag then reaches for a blue concave disc that spins around like a wheel—definitely something a baby would take amusement from, but not what she'd been hoping for. Still, she scrubs each one dutifully and leaves it to dry on the bag.

By early afternoon she is down to the final box, which is putrid and sopping. It is so soiled, Helen decides to leave the thing where it is in the fish tank. The stench reminds her of packed earth at the bottom of that disused well she tumbled into as a child.

She turns to the French door. Looks out. Lets the memory fall slack over years of untended growth.

It'll be cold soon.

Might even snow for Christmas. Helen remembers the last time she stepped out to freeze herself before a second bath; a tiny feather attached itself to one of her slippers.

And just like that, any sense of meaning she had felt would come from bringing the fish tank home is gone. Helen does not even try to reclaim it. The whole affair has been a fool's mission.

Her only thought now is to get the thing back outside—even the deep sea diver.

Long ago one just like it had belonged to her son. And herein lies the cruel paradox of human existence—not that you die, but that all happiness eventually turns against you.

5.

A NUMB FEELING PLACATES Helen as she gathers up some of the empty boxes and plastic toys from the coffee table. A moment before she drops them back into the tank, a pair of tiny eyes and a pink nose appear from a hole in the box that is smeared with muck. Calmly, Helen sets everything down on the carpet. She has never been the screaming kind, and it's not an angry face, just a small, grey cone with crooked whiskers, like every mouse in every book she ever read to David when he was little.

When she leans forward, the head drops back into the darkness of the box, which hadn't been empty after all.

Helen makes for the kitchen. Pulls open the silverware drawer then closes it again. Turns on the hot tap and turns it off. Leans on the counter. Opens the fridge without seeing any of her food bathing in the cool light. Looks at the kettle—stares at it. Her breathing quickens and there is pressure in the centre of her chest like a small button being pushed over and over.

When she eventually returns to the sitting room, everything is as she left it. The deep sea diver is dry and sits motionless on the plastic bag. Small empty boxes and toys lie at funny angles on the carpet where she dropped them. The basin of soapy water has lost its foam and cooled to murky wash.

Helen goes cautiously toward the fish tank. Leaning in, she looks into what she realises now is a bona fide mouse hole.

Although the animal doesn't appear, she can hear it faffing around, drumming the cardboard with its paws, chewing on something that makes a flicking sound.

The lonely creature is likely frightened, stranded there in a sitting room on Westminster Crescent, unaware there is someone listening, someone watching beyond the small, dark place it has come to live out the last of its days.

6.

AFTER THE LATE morning weather forecast, Helen makes a decision. She puts on her hat, coat, and shoes, still sticky from yesterday's rain.

She can't have a rodent in the place.

Absolutely not.

No.

The smell alone would be unbearable.

She roots in the cupboard for the folding umbrella. Snaps open her handbag to make sure everything is there. Takes one final look in the sitting room, where she has covered the fish tank with plastic film in case it tries to escape.

The front door closes with its usual clap of the letterbox, but Helen hesitates on the doorstep, remembering again that time she tumbled into a well not properly filled in.

For months after, fine grains of earth clung to her scalp. On the quick plummet down, her nose and mouth filled with soil. And the dark . . . so thick it was impossible to know if she'd gone blind. She cried out, of course—but each time, her voice grew smaller and smaller, until she was just a speck, then nothing beyond the churn of imagination, which placed her above like a wind, everywhere but invisible to the mother and father crunching the woods, casting their daughter's name into darkness like a small net.

Members of the police and fire brigade combed forest and field until dusk. Then, with volunteers from the veterans league and teachers union, they went all night on sugary tea and shared cigarettes.

Her father had only been back a year from the war and was teaching again at the local school, hobbling the corridors with the help of a rubber-capped walking stick. Some of the children made fun of how he walked, imitating him on the playground to make themselves laugh and feel better about their own fathers who lay at the bottom of the sea, or in pieces somewhere, soon grown over. But the other children's words and actions didn't affect Helen. So many nights she had lain still in her bed, begging God to bring her daddy home. She had even offered her life in return for his.

Deep in that wet stomach of earth, she wondered if this was the fulfillment of that bargain.

She was finally rescued in the early hours of Friday morning with the help of a neighbour's dog that had been given something of hers to smell; an embroidered handkerchief. All the searchers had to do then was follow. Her mother had tried to feed the dog but it wouldn't take anything until the child was found.

Without knowing why, Helen fumbles for her keys and strides back into the house. From a drawer between the cooker and fridge, she takes a small cutting knife. Still buttoned into her coat, Helen carries the knife into the sitting room, where she pokes six quick holes in the plastic stretched tightly over the top of the fish tank. She expects to hear or see something, but the miniature world below is perfectly silent, as though the creature knows its life is finished and has accepted it.

7.

OUTSIDE THE SKY is slate. Hard weather is coming and town is a twenty-minute slog up the hill. There, Helen hopes to find the hardware store with a person who can tell her what to do.

It doesn't rain on her walk to the shops, but the wind pulls up leaves, carrying them for as long as it can. When all this rodent business is taken care of, she will sink into a long bath. That will be her reward and with no need to torture herself by standing outside the French door in her nightie.

Helen passes the late-night shop with its white sign and gossip of pigeons. Then the long road to school, strewn with litter and a wet sock. Soon she is on Church Street, where people are frittering about the shops all wanting to get home before the weather breaks. Helen knows where she is going from an ad in the free newspaper—a place on the edge of town near the big roundabout that leads to all major roads, a truck stop, and the new Meadowpark Hospital with glass walls and artworks in the waiting area. She knows this from pictures in the weekly circular. An astrologer from *Good Morning Britain* drove up from London to cut the ribbon.

As Helen nears her destination, the street narrows and it's easy for her to imagine how it must have looked hundreds of years before, when each morning animals were herded to market along muddy tracks; then at dusk, the empty wagons rattling home past public houses where chatter and the shuffling of plates spilled into the lanes, empty but for mounds of simple dung and the imprint of hooves.

Helen remembers when there was no traffic junction or major roads. The hardware store had been a stonemason's yard, and the roundabout a bustling bottle factory and brewery. Beyond that, unploughed fields of wild grass and poppies with fence gates from the time of Waterloo and Trafalgar.

Despite a steady wind, the sweet, metallic odour of diesel enters Helen's nose from the endless stream of cars and trucks idling. Then in the distance she notices something new, the yellow sign for an American fast-food restaurant. It was a place David had loved growing up in that other country where Helen lived for sixty years. It was the only home her husband and child had ever known. Most things here would be completely foreign to them. And yet it was where she had been born and the place she had returned to now that the business of life had been settled.

A bell rings as Helen pushes open the door. A voice from somewhere inside calls to greet her, a local expression that people in major cities beyond the roundabout might have found quaint.

A round man appears wearing a smooth shop coat. His silver hair has been chopped short and there is rosiness in his cheeks from summer afternoons in the beer garden.

"I've got a mouse," she declares.

It is the first time in weeks Helen has spoken out loud.

The shopkeeper nods sympathetically, as though aware of everything that has happened to her leading up to this moment in a valley of mops and lightbulbs.

"Droppings or chewed packets in the pantry?"

"Neither," she tells the man. "I found the thing staring at me from a box it's been living in."

The shopkeeper frowns. "Brazen displays are highly unusual for *Mus musculus* and might indicate something a bit more sinister. Any froth?"

"Froth?"

"Foaming at the mouth, madam."

"Goodness no. It's a mouse, not a werewolf."

"Do you have any idea where it came from?"

Helen shuffles her feet. "I seem to have brought it in myself."

The shopkeeper perks up. "Oh, and how's that exactly?"

"Something I recently acquired."

"An antique?"

"Sort of."

"Auction houses are notorious . . . *no-torious* . . . for infestations. We must now ask ourselves, could there be more than one, as mice are usually quite social by nature."

Helen shrugs. "Don't they all look the same?"

"To the untrained eye, certainly. But usually the scale of the infestation is apparent not by the frequency of sightings, but the volume of waste."

"Waste?"

The man puts together his thumb and finger, trapping a few centimetres of air. "Droppings, madam. Though male mice tend to be loners, especially in youth, so if you don't hear much activity, and don't see too many droppings, it's likely just one little boy."

Helen remembers the noise that woke her up. "What does a person normally do in this situation, I mean to remove the animal?"

"There's only one thing to do," says the shopkeeper, drawing a finger across his neck.

Helen opens her handbag and closes it again without looking inside.

"I can't just put it in the garden?" she asks, wondering why she hadn't thought of such a thing before. That would have saved her a trip to town.

"There's no law against it . . ." says the man. "But if the animal has developed a fondness for your home, it's going to find a way back in. Mark my words, they can sausage their bodies through even the tiniest gaps." The shopkeeper turns and Helen follows him to a wall of devices sealed in brightly coloured packets.

"We have your traditional mousetrap with snap mechanism, packets of poison . . . though that often leads to the animal dying in a wall and stinking up the place. Glue traps are your best bet."

"How do they work?"

"The animal walks on it, then gets stuck."

"And that ends its life?"

"No, no, it'll be alive when you find it—but this way you don't have to deal with the bloody entrails of the traditional snap-trap system."

Helen leans toward a large packet of glue traps.

"That's a family pack of three," says the man, taking it down and inspecting a sticker on the back. "Obviously the creature won't be dead when you discover it . . . usually in the morning . . . but the glue is industrial strength so any animal stuck will never get free, no matter how much it panics. You just pick up the trap, on a spade if you prefer, and drop it in your bin outside. It will die of fright or starve to death in a few days."

Helen exhales. Everything that is happening now, she has brought on herself. She takes the bag of glue traps from the man and pretends to inspect it.

The shopkeeper slips both hands into his pockets. "I think most people just whack it with a shoe in the region of its head. That's the quickest way once it's stuck."

"Don't you have anything that allows a person to capture it live?"

The shopkeeper rubs his nose. "I can order them, but it could take a week. As I said, unless you drive it to the ends of the earth, it'll probably find a way back inside. You could be catching and releasing the same mouse for months. The little fella might start to think it's a game."

Helen is tired now. "No, no. I want it gone."

"Just set the trap against the baseboard or in the food cupboard and wait. You'll know when you've got him."

"How?"

"Oh the ruckus they cause trying to pull free! Some of them even scream."

Helen frowns. "I don't like the sound of that. I might be in bed."

"If you're lucky, he'll have a heart attack there and then on the glue board."

Helen goes lightheaded, quite unsteady on her feet. She wonders if she'll fall, whacking her own head on a low shelf as both legs buckle.

The shopkeeper drops the glue traps and raises his hands in readiness. "Steady now, missus, you're having a spell!"

The whole thing lasts only a few seconds, but Helen feels her eyes almost shut.

Before leaving the shop, she apologizes and tells the shopkeeper that she's fine, completely fine. "It was really nothing," she says, "most likely the weather or not having eaten enough for breakfast"—no need to mention her husband, Len, who pawed at his chest then went sideways off his chair during Sunday lunch on the terrace.

It really was that quick.

By the time they had finished what was in their mouths he was gone.

8.

HELEN IS PASSING through the center of town on her way back when it starts to pour.

A limp plastic bag hangs from the sinewy fingers of one hand. Inside are glue traps, her handbag, and a plunger she had noticed on sale beside the till. The wooden handle sticks out from the bag and makes her think of Pinocchio's nose. Helen roots around for her umbrella, then remembers setting it down on the hall table after going back into the house.

"Bugger!" she snaps, angry at herself for bringing somebody else's rubbish into her sitting room on Westminster Crescent.

Not wanting to get soaked, Helen ducks into a covered market and stands near a curved glass cabinet, packed with slabs of fudge. She shakes the rain off her bag and pulls a foot out of one shoe to see if her tights are wet. A girl asks if she would like something. Helen says she is only there on account of the weather, and shuffles off. She *had* wanted something, but after being asked her desire felt foolish and vain.

The next shop has a window of toys glowing under electric light. Helen stands there taking it in. There are teddy bears, dollhouses, spinning tops, jigsaw puzzles, fire trucks, Lego sets, dinosaurs, and battery-operated cars with rubber wheels.

David would have loved this place. Heavens above, it would have been an argument for sure.

As she lingers, it isn't any particular memory that comes, just random things, like the way he pulled her hand, even when she said no he couldn't have it; he would lean his small body into hers—not to get his way, but to reassure her of something they never said out loud.

Other memories circle overhead, waiting for her to choose. Instead, she steps out onto the wet stones and trudges home, fudge-less.

Helen drops her plastic bag just inside the front door, where linoleum becomes carpet. The bag sits upright because of the plunger. She takes off her shoes and places them on the mat beneath the bone dry umbrella. Her tights are soaked. She hangs her coat from a high peg and imagines the small puddle that will form underneath.

A moment later the radio is on. Words enter the kitchen as she fills the electric kettle. A group of people have blown up another group of people; an iceberg is melting faster than experts had hoped it would; somebody who tells fortunes on the television is dead after an unexpected accident; an argument between countries about who can fish where has escalated to a standoff hundreds of miles out to sea.

None of this has any effect on her. It is no longer Helen's world to worry about. And in her mind it is the same news over and over again, with the only difference being that people think they're hearing it for the first time.

She carries her mug upstairs. Turns on the bath. Sips the scalding tea as ropes of water splatter into the tub. It is obvious to her now what will happen with the thing downstairs. The trip to town has been a complete waste of time, with the exception of her new plunger for the occasional turd that spins instead of going down.

After screwing closed the taps, Helen removes each piece of damp clothing and steps gingerly into the clear liquid. Immediately, a deep warmth radiates to her core. Who could have known that in advanced age, sensual pleasure would come from sitting in a plastic tub of hot water like some tropical insect?

The radio is still on and Helen can hear the swell of an orchestra.

After the bath Helen lies on her bed in a towel—not to sleep but to ease the pressure in her legs from the long walk. When hunger gnaws, she gets into her nightclothes and tramps downstairs. Helen assumes it's around six o'clock, but it is actually eight o'clock. The street outside is still wet from the afternoon rain. When she turns off the radio, a cloak of silence falls over the house.

It's too late for dinner, so Helen takes some bread, fish paste, and a knife. Boils an egg. Cuts the sandwich twice to make four pieces. Chews each square slowly, watching curls of steam rise from the pot. Jostled by the boil, the egg knocks and Helen wonders if the mouse is hungry and can smell her own small meal. She slides her coupon book across the kitchen counter. Reads the conditions of sale written in small letters at the bottom of each rectangle—just above the scissor line. She shells her egg under the cold tap. Eats it with a knife and fork. When that's done, Helen washes everything. Leaves it to dry on a tea towel. Wipes the counter with a sponge. Tosses the water. Rinses the pot and turns it over to drain.

Helen hasn't been in the sitting room since getting back from town because she doesn't want to see it or hear it. But now she stands over the tank, arms on her hips, waiting—perhaps even hoping for some sign that will justify her next action.

She wonders if she should put on the television, but the sound of applause or music might summon the creature onto its cardboard stage like some tiny late-night host.

Outside, the wind pushes at things in its way. Best to get it over with, Helen concedes, striding over to the French door. She fiddles with the lock then throws the thing open. A tongue of cold curls past her, but Helen hurries back to the table, lifting the tank in one motion and rushing out to the wild overgrowth, where she sets it down on a patio square, as if making her final move in a game. She rips off the punctured plastic wrap. Turns and scurries back in to gather the empty boxes and colourful plastic things. Drops them on the patio stones beside the aquarium with a satisfying grunt.

Back inside Helen locks the door, panting from the effort.

There.

It's over.

The thing is free and no harm has been done. The tank can stay on the patio forever for all she cares.

Helen marches through to the kitchen. Opens the fridge. Decides to celebrate her good sense, not with lemonade but a container of lactose-free yoghurt. The kind with a foil lid and syrupy fruit at the bottom. She takes it into the sitting room with a spoon that came free inside a box of cornflakes two years ago at Easter. Turns on the television. Puts her feet up on the coffee table. It is Saturday night, after all, and there are many good programmes. Helen flicks between stations but can't choose. As she doesn't want her snack to end before getting into something, she puts down the remote and settles on some BBC drama about an old woman.

Close to ten, Helen feels her eyes wanting to close. She forces herself off the couch. Carries the empty yoghurt container and spoon to the kitchen. Rinses the spoon. Washes out the plastic pot in a stream of warm water.

Before turning off the lights and going up the stairs to her bed, Helen goes over the day's excursion. Just to be safe, she takes a pair of scissors into the hall. Reaches into the still-wet bag for the glue traps. Stands over the coffee table in the sitting room. Cuts along the marked edge. Carefully removes two of the traps from their protective sleeves. Placing them strategically on the carpet near the French door, Helen recalls what the man in the hardware store said about the thing coming in and trying to make itself at home.

There is no reason to feel bad now. None at all.

She has given it a chance to escape and return to where it belongs—those small hidden places of life where no one thinks to look. The creature is simply a product of some other world, marooned by time and circumstances, a castaway on Westminster Crescent.

9.

During the night, a thick band of low pressure snaps over the town. The house creaks as though something is trying to uproot it. Between growls of thunder, the curtains flash like bared teeth. Outside, garden furniture is being rearranged like pieces in a board game.

Lying there in bed with her feet touching, Helen wonders if windows ever blow in. Pictures herself lifting squares of cardboard into the holes.

She turns her body to the wall, hoping to sink again, but rain is lashing the panes. She remembers a book her father used to read at bedtime about a lonely lighthouse keeper. She knew the story by heart, but always wondered how the old woman had come to be living in the lighthouse. There was nothing in the words or the pictures about that. Helen dwells upon her childish wish to reach the old woman and let her know there were people on the other side of the story—if only she could look out from the page she would see them.

Helen turns over. Fumbles with the lamp on her bedside table. Warm in bed, held in place by the drumming rain, she is beyond harm. She thinks then of the fish tank in the back garden. Broods over what could be happening. It *must* have escaped by now. Hasn't she given it every opportunity to leave its ruined world and seek out something better for the time it has left?

But if the creature has not ventured out, either through fear or hopelessness—the tank will be filling up. Surely it has jumped out. Mice are known for their gymnastic feats. Helen tries to remember the height of the sides when she held the tank in both arms.

She senses her father again. But unlike Orpheus she knows not to look with her eyes.

There he is now. In the hall with the lighthouse story book in one hand. Ready to hoist her from the well. Helen imagines his ship.

There it is now. Between the dusk and the deep blue. Moments before torpedoes peel open the hull.

To the Spanish fishermen who found him bobbing, unconscious on the current, he was just a young sailor—not a father, or a husband, or an only son.

For years after, he wrote to the fishermen—sent small, Kodak pictures of his wife and daughter in the garden, wearing sunglasses at the beach, washing the car on Saturday with rags drawn from a steel bucket. Then on Christmas at the table with silly hats and glasses of sherry, the rubber-capped walking stick stowed safely under his chair.

Helen throws back the wave of her covers. Pulls on her tartan slippers. Going down, the floorboards creak as if woken. She flicks on the hall light. Wades through the dark sitting room to the French door.

While the thunder has ceased, the rain is insistent.

Helen can't see the fish tank at all. The glass of the French door is black with silvery eyes. As the downpour intensifies to a higher octave, Helen takes a deep breath. Jiggles the lock. Steps out onto the stage as cold burrows into her nightclothes. Icy drops splash against her scalp. She takes a few steps toward the tank and can see it is starting to fill. The box is there, soft and sagging, but no sign of the creature. Helen expects it is somewhere in the bushes, dry and sheltered, laughing into its paw.

To be sure, she bends down. Grips the glass. Turns the whole thing on its side. A freezing torrent of slimy water rushes out over the tops of her slippers.

"Bugger!" she cries, back-stepping to the house.

Safely inside, she locks the door—but when reaching to pull the curtain her left slipper comes down on something mushy.

Helen freezes. *How could it have managed to . . . ?*

Then she realises.

"Buggering hell!"

Trying to maneuver her now vastly elongated foot—she steps on the other trap.

In a blaze of anger she claps her way across the kitchen like a demented clown. Fuming at the toaster, Helen grabs the coupon book, rolls it up, and begins whacking her feet repeatedly in a vain attempt to be free of her wretched circumstances.

SUNDAY

10.

IT IS ALMOST noon when Helen gets up the following day. Feeling for slippers at the side of the bed, she remembers her late-night battle with the coupon book.

Going down, Helen notices how worn the carpet is under bare feet.

She flicks on the radio, then enters the kitchen, where she is confronted by the sight of her tartan slippers each cemented to a glue trap. There is a trail of dirt with bits of decaying leaf and small twigs.

With calm remorse, Helen fills the kettle then nips to the downstairs loo for some toilet paper. It is a tiny room and always damp, but using it occasionally spares her the journey upstairs.

She wipes the kitchen floor then goes into the sitting room. The carpet there is quite bad where she stepped back inside from the patio. It isn't just leaves, but clumps of green and brown matter. She returns to the kitchen for a cloth rag soaked in hot water. On her hands and knees cleaning, Helen spies movement on the other side of the glass.

It's the mouse—perched atop the grimy box that washed out when she dropped the tank on its side. For something so small, it certainly has presence. It is on both back legs with two paws pressed under its chin like a medieval supplicant.

So low as to be scorned without a sin, she remembers from school. *Without offence to God cast out of view . . .*

Helen motions at the creature through the glass. "There's a nice bush over there. Out of the wind. Go on, shoo!" The sound of her own voice startles her, as though somebody else is speaking.

The mouse twists its head in the wrong direction.

"Not there, you fool! Over there! The green thing with leaves."

When the mouse turns back, Helen wonders if it's merely seeing its own reflection that it has mistaken for another mouse of similar temperament. She leans in to the glass, so close that her breath becomes visible.

"I've given you every chance to escape and don't know why you're doing this. Get away while you still can."

On the other side of the window, the mouse opens and closes its mouth repeatedly as though copying her. It reminds Helen of a common pond fish.

When she stands, the mouse flashes into its box through the hole.

"So it saw me," she says, going quickly into the hall. There is one trap left in the plastic bag. She could place it beside his box this time. Perhaps with something on it. A seed? A crisp? A smear of margarine? She has no idea what mice enjoy.

Then Helen has a thought. *Why not put on shoes and just move the box to the hedge?*

That's what David would have told her to do.

She imagines him there, leaning on the counter in a T-shirt and long shorts. He pushes up his glasses and looks around. Studies the things that fill his mother's life in his absence. Helen stops what she is doing. Lets memory shuffle the deck. They are now in the kitchen of their old house in Australia. It's the last week of school. No sound in this one, but she knows they're talking about final exams. He pushes his glasses up and Helen says that on Saturday after work, she's driving him to the optician in Westfield to have the frames tightened. He doesn't want to go. Tells her it's his only form of exercise. They laugh at that. He chooses an apple from the bowl and rubs it on his shorts. In a few months he'll be at the university and moments like this will keep her going. She'll want to telephone every day, but knows she shouldn't, for he must learn to live without her.

Helen lays both palms on the counter. Smiles at the kettle. Oh, the irony of it all. You can burn all the photos and scrapbooks and report cards and certificates, but in the end they find their way back.

She would do what David said. Just go out and move the box over to the hedge. No need for bloodshed or more glue.

But first, a cup of tea.

Some toast. An apple quartered.

And perhaps an hour or two of telly? *Antiques Roadshow* might be on.

There really is no urgency. It's Sunday, and the thing is probably quite busy itself after the rain, salvaging whatever bits and pieces it has left.

As long as she goes before dark. She wants everything settled by then.

11.

BY LATE AFTERNOON, God is everywhere. Choristers from Aberdeen on BBC One, while ITV is broadcasting interviews with people from different faiths about prayers they know by heart and rely on during hard times.

Helen has not set foot in a house of worship for decades. The last time was David's service, attended by almost the entire school where he was head teacher. A few of the children couldn't keep still. They fiddled with toys or just played with their fingers.

Helen admires the sober herd before her on television. Sitting quietly in rows, their faces stilled by the echo of shoes over ancient stone. One by one they take their turn at the front with the body of Christ and a wetting of wine-as-blood on the lips. They must have been told not to look at the camera so that people at home might believe they are there, with them.

When it is time to pray, Helen closes her eyes with the others. Lets her head drop. She does not wish for anything, but hopes her presence might be felt in whichever corner of the universe belongs to her.

When she opens her eyes, candles are being lit by children in white gowns. No sound at all as each wick blooms to fire. The television is also a candle. It flickers and flames in the dusk.

During the final hymn, credits appear on the screen, obscuring the faces of those still in song. Helen watches their mouths open and close. This reminds her of something she has to do.

While putting her shoes on, she notices her empty pie box from Friday still on the counter. She opens a drawer. Pulls a clean knife. Cuts a small hole in the top of the cardboard. When this is done, Helen closes the flaps on the side of the box so there is only one way to get in and out. In the downstairs loo she rips a few squares of paper. Drops them into the hole she has made. The nights will soon be sharp with cold. She can already sense its claws, scratching at the doors and windows.

On the patio, Helen looks down at the old wet box. Clears her throat to tell the animal she is near. When nothing stirs or appears in the hole, she scoops it up. Hurries to the overgrown hedge. Sets it down beside the new pie box in her other hand. There is little weight difference between the boxes, and so Helen suspects the soiled one is empty. The creature must have vanished that afternoon, and is now somewhere with its own kind, their plush bodies tumbling over one another for warmth and play.

Once both boxes are positioned, Helen pushes the new one a few inches under the hedge in case there is more rain overnight.

"It doesn't get much better than this," she says.

But stepping into the house she realises it could be better. The creature had opened and closed its mouth when she saw it through the French door. A mother is fluent in signs like that. Under stark kitchen light, Helen hunts for anything small enough to fit such a tiny hole. Then she remembers her baking tin. Inside is a loose mountain of oats. Helen takes a pinch then hurries back outside. There is no sign of life and side by side the boxes look like bits of recycling that have blown away. Regardless of the creature's whereabouts, Helen sprinkles the hard tongues of oat, making sure some drop through the crudely fashioned hole in the pie box.

If the mouse has gone away, she thinks, leaving food might bring it back. She remembers the words of the man in the hardware store, warning her about making the thing "feel at home."

She locks the French door and pulls the curtain. It is just one meal. And somewhere dry to sleep. As a child her father always told her, *Do your best.* Helen can hear him now, as if he were just behind a door, about to come in for his tea.

The bathtub fills quickly with steam and water. Helen folds a towel to set at one end as a pillow. She sheds her clothes and gets in. It isn't late, but she's already eaten, as it's Sunday. Lord knows she needs a good night. Monday is when the shopping gets done. Walking to the supermarket is manageable. But the slog home with stuffed bags pulling on her arms, cutting into fingers? Helen imagines herself a grim figure, hunched over, clopping along.

Mondays, however, are redeemed by the two o'clock film, for which she buys herself a Bakewell tart.

Once in her nightgown, Helen shoulders the bedroom curtain. A car is parked between streetlights. There are two people inside talking. The engine and headlamps are off. They wear coats and turn in their seats from time to time, as though desperate to be understood.

In bed, the sheets sigh as Helen seeks a position of stillness. The radiators will have to go on soon, otherwise ice will form on the inside of the windows. That happened last winter. Helen woke in puffs of her own breath like a dragon.

The passage ahead to Monday seems clear, and Helen can feel sleep like a weight pulling. But then a scream from outside and she's sitting up. At first she believes it's the woman from the car. But then another scream tears across her bedroom like invisible fire. Helen knows what it is. She's heard it before. The first time, she thought it was a baby. But then the cry rose to something unmistakably feline.

Helen falls back on the bed. The pleasantness of Sunday has come apart and lies in pieces at the feet of Monday. She closes her eyes. Exhales. Goes limp. Waits for the next current of sleep to carry her out.

But the cries persist, whipping at her like pieces of loose string.

If only she had turned her back that night in the street, just walked away from the glistening tank and pile of bags. She could have taken a bath and drifted far, far away from the steel jaws of the rubbish lorry grinding the glass and wet boxes to pulp. She would not have known of the life inside. Felt nothing as the tiny flame went out.

MONDAY

12.

AT THE BOTTOM of the stairs in a web of street light, Helen finds her shoes and puts them on. Once through the kitchen, she jiggles the French door and goes out, feeling a sense of déjà vu. But in the darkness, everything is wild and unfamiliar. Shivering just beyond the open door she hears the animal hiss, like hot steel plunged in water. The dirty box and the pie box are exactly where she has left them. Helen leans in, scanning the ground for a small, torn body, or evidence of a struggle. It is quite possible the cat has taken it whole, to be dropped later in a soft, stiff heap where the cat's owner will see it.

An act of love made possible by an act of violence.

Helen recoils in disgust. Isn't this the grand hypocrisy from which we cannot reconcile God and free ourselves? She remembers the people on television belting out hymns. They seem foolish to her now.

It is so cold that she can't stop her body from shaking. She wonders if the cat is watching from a tree or fence post, scared by the slide of a door but biding its time to resume the hunt.

There is a chance the mouse is long gone and asleep somewhere dry, with no idea of what's taking place on its behalf. Helen's hands prickle with cold. There really is nothing left to do now but pick up both boxes and bring them inside.

Once the French door is sealed against danger, the house seems especially quiet, as though each room is holding its breath.

Helen hovers over the sink. The two boxes are most likely empty, but she takes another pinch of oats, which fall like a shower of small stones.

Trudging back upstairs to bed, she recalls the singing on television. The mouths opening and closing with more faith than certainty.

When, as a child, she would get low, Helen's mother used to sing hymns and pet her hair. Some of the words were lovely. Helen undresses to her own gentle music and gets into bed. The moon is out and anything in its path already drenched.

13.

IN THE MORNING, Helen lies motionless with her eyes open. If the two boxes in her sink are empty, the day will simply be a normal Monday. She will throw them out, wipe clean the sink, and that will be that.

If not, then a decision will have to be arrived at.

When she gets downstairs routine takes over. Passing through the hall, she flicks on the radio. Next stop is the kettle, which she lifts from its cradle to fill. But halfway to the sink she freezes. The mouse is on its back legs munching a piece of oat as though playing a small harmonica. When it spots her, the creature stops eating and fumbles with the food in its paws. Helen has never seen a rodent up close, and is surprised by the softness of its coat. She had expected the animal's fur to be matted with clumps of filth, but the soft waves are clean and brushed. Its ears are huge—elephantine—but also translucent, with delicate branches of blood vessels.

When she has gotten over the surprise, Helen backtracks to the downstairs loo, where she fills the kettle without any idea of what to do beyond making a cup of tea. While she is setting the kettle in its cradle, the mouse moves to the edge of the pie box. After reaching out a paw to touch the metal, it shuffles down off the box, scuttling over to the plug, where it drinks from a pool of drips that have collected overnight.

When the kettle boils, the click of the button sends the mouse flying back through the hole of his new pie box. Helen reaches into the sink. Picks up his old, filthy home. Drops it in the bin with some semblance of a smile.

She brews the tea. Opens the bin again. Watches the hot bag plunge toward the box given up by the creature for the one she provided. Then into the cup go two sugars. A gulp of milk. A spoon.

With the first sip, Helen opens the fridge again. Removes a bottle of lemonade that is almost empty. Unscrews the cap and carries it to the downstairs loo. After rinsing, she fills it with a few drops of water. Cautiously, Helen lowers the cap to the sink. Waits. Watches. When nothing happens, she ferries her tea to the sitting room, where she can enjoy it without any fear of the mouse coming out and doing something else.

One thing Helen can't understand is why it isn't more afraid. How has such a small, soft, trusting creature survived in this harsh world? She takes a few sips of tea. Listens for the radio. But it isn't music, just voices too low to hear. There must be something in gentleness, she ponders, some great power that people just aren't aware of. Not wishing to dwell on the live animal in her sink, Helen plucks the remote from between two cushions. But it's still those annoying breakfast talk shows, with people on couches talking absolute nonsense.

When she goes back to the kitchen Helen can hear the mouse in its pie box, and through the hole sees a flash of white, which must be the toilet paper getting moved. *It's getting ready for bed*, she supposes, *after having dined and drunk its fill.* She inspects the lemonade cap, but can't tell if it's been touched.

When the scratching stops, Helen takes a pad of paper from the drawer where she keeps foil, wax paper, string, and any coupons cut from the magazine that comes free with the paper. A pen lives on the left side of the bread bin.

She boils the kettle again and makes toast, wondering if the smell will draw the creature out. She ventures to imagine what it's like in there. *Do mice close their eyes when sleeping?* She knows they curl into a ball. A lot of creatures do that. Breathing slows, too, just like in humans.

Back on the couch with her second cup of tea and now toast, the radio is thundering out Beethoven's *Pastoral*. Helen again tries to decide what to do, but can think of nothing beyond her list. It's a Monday, after all. And that's when the shopping gets done.

Radio Times
Grapes—if taut
Three new potatoes
Three carrots
Two parsnips or a nice little swede
Peas frozen
Tea
Lemonade
Yoghurt
Eggs
Double Gloucester

Milk
Toilet paper?
Bread
Bakewell tart
Cream crackers
Digestives

Helen writes things in the order she will find them on her route around the supermarket. She has enough margarine for another two weeks and three rolls of toilet paper in the airing cupboard. She isn't taking any medicine, nor does she need any creams, powders, tonics, or lozenges. The only real proof of her advanced age are a chronic, persistent feeling of defeat, aching limbs, and the power of invisibility to anyone between the ages of ten and fifty.

She would like to buy more vegetables in tins, save herself the hassle of washing and cutting, but they simply can't be carried with her legs the way they are. And taking a taxi would mean talking. Being asked questions that rattle the doors she keeps locked.

14.

THE SUPERMARKET IS a twenty-minute slog up the hill, then ten minutes through the old haymarket. Passing the school, Helen smells cooked food and imagines the pupils in disorderly rows filling themselves with potatoes and gravy, apple pie and lumpy custard.

Beyond that is the kindergarten, where cries and footfalls echo from the playground. As Helen walks by, a hand bell is swung by the teacher and small knots of children come undone.

She goes further, turns right at the library and then left into an alley at the Butcher's Arms. At the end of Magdalen Road, Helen stops at the crossing. Stares into the knuckled arms of an oak as wind gallops through branches. Some leaves fall while others cling to the memory of a summer past.

When she is almost there, Helen stops. Cannot recall placing the list in her purse. But once her handbag is open, there it is between the coins like a tongue. She feels afraid then, by this sudden drama with the mouse. Her home has been invaded.

But what was she supposed to do? The lone creature doesn't seem to belong anywhere. Any family is long gone and most likely forgotten by the way it darts in and out of the pie box, its small spirit undimmed by fear and circumstance. Perhaps on the walk home she will know what action to take.

Helen undoes the buttons on her coat. Yanks the red handle of a trolley to separate it noisily from another. After peeling the *Radio Times* from a stack near the Christmas decorations, Helen threads the bright aisles, collecting the things on her list as tills beep in the distance. Workers in white gowns stuff chillers with packages of meat, Scotch eggs, and savoury pies. Helen pulls over to inspect a tray of herb-infused sausages squashed flat behind the plastic. She imagines the sizzle of salty fingers curling through her house. After turning the container in her hands she puts it back. So often she has bought something she believes would be nice, only to get home and find her appetite has thinned.

Her weekly Bakewell tart, however, is the exception.

As Helen nears the in-store bakery, her tired heart quickens at the sight of two remaining tarts in the glass cabinet. There is only one other person ahead of her—a young man who, to Helen's relief, is pointing at something on the lower shelf: a blackberry napoleon that looks sickly.

When it's Helen's turn, she notices the girl behind the counter is wearing a red linen apron that is much too big, as though it were meant for somebody else. Perhaps the girl is new and undergoing a trial period? Or she has forgotten her apron at home after a night of arguing with her husband over comments his mother made? Or did something spill as she served an elderly father his porridge? Having been alone for so long, Helen finds relief in small imaginary dramas.

With her Bakewell tart safely stowed, Helen peers around at the other shoppers filling their trolleys with jars and packages. Then she recalls her own drama—a stray animal is living in her kitchen sink waiting for her to come home. It might even be hungry and smell the food in her bags as she steps in, knackered from the long walk. Often in moments of indecision, Helen will hear the voices of Len or David or Mum or Dad, just beyond the reach of her eyes. But this time Helen feels quite alone, as though anything new in life comes at the expense of something past.

The last stop before checkout is the dried goods section, from which Helen draws one sleeve of digestive biscuits. Impulsively, she parks her trolley and returns to where there are small packets of unsalted party nuts on hooks at the end of the aisle. She has her tart and her biscuits—why shouldn't the mouse get something, too? Its life is most likely nearing the end—as only an elderly mouse with nothing to lose could be so trusting and grateful.

On her way to the till, Helen bumps into a display with fake grass and containers of strawberries piled high.

No, she thinks. *Just no.*

It has party nuts. That's enough.

Years ago, she would have brought one package home. Rinsed them in the sink with a swirling motion. Cut the tops. Quartered the larger ones into a bowl then carried it into his room. David would be at his books. Without looking up, he would reach into the bowl and pluck the first piece he touched.

Helen would just stand there. *Thanks, Mum,* she would say sarcastically.

You're welcome, he would reply, still glued to a book, but smiling now.

It was one of their jokes.

"Oh bugger it," Helen says, reaching for a container. The threat feels distant this time, as though the present is occupied with something the past can't shift.

When it's her turn at the till, she puts the things from her trolley onto the moving belt. Follows each item with a sense she has done her best. After all, it might not be around to see another summer, so why not give it one final taste of what it meant to live?

15.

AT HOME, HELEN drops her bag of shopping on the kitchen counter beside the bread bin. The mouse is lying on its pie box, chewing cardboard around the hole. It has elongated its body and appears to Helen like a sausage in a fur coat. The cap of lemonade is down by half, so things have been happening in her absence. Helen wonders if the creature knows the cap has been put there on purpose. She is quite sure now it is a boy mouse. Not only by the way he's chewing noisily, but from the small packet between his back legs where the fur is a darker shade and there are two distinct lumps.

She opens the refrigerator and makes space for the new items, somewhat amazed at how calm she feels with a wild animal in her kitchen sink.

When all the food is put away, Helen glances at the oven clock. Only eighteen minutes before the afternoon film on BBC Two. She picks a juicy bell from the container of strawberries, rinses it in the downstairs loo, and cuts a tiny wedge on the chopping board. When Helen drops it a few centimetres from the creature's tail, the mouse turns and grabs the morsel. Standing up on his back legs, he turns the piece around and around in both paws as though choosing where to bite first. *It must be a familiar taste*, Helen thinks, *something it knows, which means that mice remember what has happened to them—just like people*. Helen stares in wonder as the mouse opens his mouth wide enough for her to spy a pink tongue and two minuscule rows of teeth—just dots really.

Helen puts her empty shopping bags in a low cupboard, then fills the kettle from the downstairs loo.

With only six minutes to go before the film, she ferries her tea and Bakewell tart into the sitting room on a tray. The afternoon has turned mild with a high, fast wind. Soft hunks of cloud open to arms of light that reach for things in her garden. The toys and empty boxes are still there on the green patio stones, as is the tipped aquarium, which rests on its side like a sunken ship.

On the couch, Helen tucks her feet under a cushion. Her legs ache from the morning walk, and she remembers her tartan slippers, still glued to the boards at one end of the kitchen.

To her utter delight, the film is black and white—a proper picture. Helen turns up the volume to hear the crackle. How she loved those Saturday mornings with her mother strolling to the Odeon, where there was always a queue. Many of the faces lining up she recognized from school—though everyone looked different out of uniform, as if already part of the adult world they were destined for. The children must have felt it, too, on account of how quietly they waited for the blind to roll up in the ticket booth. Many of their fathers had not come back from the war, and for this reason Helen's mother always accompanied her to buy the ticket. Common decency was important in those days. Many had died for it.

Helen nibbles her Bakewell tart as the music fades and the film opens with a woman picking flowers at the base of a stone wall. Someone calls her name and she turns to the camera. Helen remembers when her own hair was long and rich with colour. Len used to let it fall through his fingers like cascading water. It wasn't long after the dance that she wrote home to say she had met someone, and with her parents' blessing, a date would be set.

The actress is now walking alone in an orchard. This is going to be a good story—Helen can feel it.

About halfway through, with the tart almost eaten, the tea drunk, and the fate of an entire family in the hands of a heroine now lost at sea, Helen realises she has to do something with the mouse. She can't keep using the downstairs loo. The basin is too small for washing up, the floor is cold, and there's a damp, murky light that depresses her.

The animal and his box will have to be moved. But where?

With the heroine waving madly at a distant ship, Helen thinks of the neighbour's cat, who most likely knows the mouse's last known whereabouts. So he definitely cannot go back outside, as all the fellow seems interested in is chomping strawberries and going to bed.

Does he not understand this world is a place of danger and suffering? And what if he's diseased? Wasn't London overrun in 1665 by rodents carrying fatal diseases? They're like figures of Greek tragedy, Helen muses, *doomed to suffer by fickle powers.*

At least the shopping is done.

Helen takes a bite of her cake, savoring that moment on her tongue when the icing mixes with pastry.

When the film is over she lies back. Her eyes are closing. She could fall asleep but is held in place by an interesting thought. Could there be a wildlife center that could send someone in a white van to pick him up?

They might have proper places for mice to live out their last weeks or months with other mice. Or perhaps they could train him to live in the wild? Wasn't that where animals belonged?

Helen feels warm satisfaction and melts into a doze. A few hours later she wakes in the arms of the six o'clock news, which means the window for supper is closing. Helen flicks on the kitchen light but there's no sign of the mouse. Most likely sleeping off the strawberry. She will surrender the rest of them to the wildlife person. Who knows if such places have a budget for expensive fruit. They could even be shared with the other mice. That would help him make friends.

The oven clicks to life, and Helen clomps a frozen pie onto a baking pan. When it's in, she looks at the box in her hands. A white farmhouse nestled in a green valley with a thread of smoke rising up to the barcode. Helen imagines a person like herself inhabiting the cottage and the many animals hidden in the hills and vales, the way dreams are hidden in the folds of sleep.

This pie box is larger than the other container. It gives Helen an idea. If the animal is going to a wildlife centre, it might be a good thing to feed it up, as there is probably no guarantee of regular mealtimes once it gets there. What if it's like *Wentworth*, the prison drama? Albeit a mouse version. And how long the triage of new arrivals might take is anybody's guess. The facility is likely staffed entirely by volunteers—who in Helen's experience are often useless.

As hot air swells the cooking pie, Helen takes a whole strawberry from the container, a bit of bread crust, some oats, and an unsalted nut. She cuts the fruit and bread. Breaks the nut and oats with her fingers. Rips a square of fresh toilet paper from the downstairs loo. Arranges the items in a small pile. Returns to the downstairs loo to fill a saucepan with water. Sets it on the ring to boil. Pours in frozen peas. Waits.

When the pie is ready, Helen turns the oven off. Lowers the door with heat pushing against her face. She removes the pot from the stovetop. Strains the peas in the downstairs loo. Tumbles them from the colander onto the plate beside the steaming pie.

When Helen lifts the toilet paper of mouse food, it tips and the pieces go flying. Without picking them up, she throws open the cutlery drawer. Grabs a knife and fork. Storms into the sitting room with her own plate of supper.

On the television is a family drama set on a farm. The food sits steaming on her lap, but instead of eating, Helen stares at her old, unreliable hands. Not a soul alive would have believed the miraculous things they were once capable of.

She tries to focus on the television but the voices seem far away, as if unconnected to her life now on Westminster Crescent—and even farther from the one in Australia that she never realised would end the way it did.

Helen sets her untouched plate of supper on the coffee table and gets up. If anybody threw food at her like that, she wouldn't touch it either—even if she were starving. She imagines herself arguing with the man in the hardware store about the dignity of mice. *Look* . . . she would say, pointing to fur on his belly . . . *it doesn't clean and brush itself. HE does it, with his own two paws and tongue* . . .

When she gets to the kitchen there's no sign of him.

In the downstairs loo Helen rips another piece of toilet paper, which she lays flat in the sink. Then carefully, she collects every crumb, fragment, and blob, arranging the pieces neatly on the white square. It looks pretty when she's finished and Helen is glad she got up to do it. Before returning to the couch, she glances into the pie box, where a grey head with long whiskers is peering out through the hole.

Its eyes are like two currants, but bright with something she has seen before, in the faces of those who now haunt her.

16.

HELEN LINGERS IN the bath. Eyes closing. Limbs wrapped with heat. Another Monday has come and gone but this one has been . . . peculiar.

In the bedroom, she pulls her nightgown off the radiator and readies for bed. It isn't late but the house is quiet and will stay that way until morning. She peels back the covers. Lets her head sink into the pillow. Reaches for the lamp.

Since returning to the town of her childhood, Helen has often wondered what day she will go. She positions her feet under the bedclothes so they are touching. If tonight, she hopes it will come swiftly. Wash her away without any fuss.

A moment before drifting off, a terrible thought occurs to her.

Helen opens her eyes and sits up.

If she dies in the night, *he* will be alone. The lemonade cap will be licked dry within a day. The food won't last much longer. And with no way out of the sink to help himself, it will be a worse fate than if she'd left the creature outside at the mercy of rain and the neighbour's cat.

Reality is all corners and sharp edges. Then a more unsettling truth drops: Helen is no longer able to die.

What she has both wanted and feared for so long is now impossible. Squeezing both fists, she turns sharply to the bedside table. "It's like having a baby! At eighty-three!"

As if loosened by anger, a memory drifts toward her like a small feather: she *has* seen the toys outside on the patio stones before. At the pet shop in Westfield. She was with David. A few days before his thirteenth birthday. They had gone to choose the aquarium for his room. The toys were on a shelf beside the cages. She can't remember why they were looking at them, but they were stacked in rows with stickers that displayed the price. Those exact things. A wheel. A tube. A blue castle with turrets and air holes at each corner.

So the deep sea diver *had* been part of a set, after all.

Helen wonders what else she can't remember, and why memory holds things back. The bigger question is why all this is happening now. Could what we call coincidence be something intended, with a meaning purposely hidden? That would imply design. A God. But what sort of God would strike down a boy's father during Sunday lunch? Then allow the boy to grow into a beautiful, gentle man, only to snatch him, too?

If there is *something*, Helen ponders, *and it's not malicious but loving—then it must be very small and at times powerless, rather like the mouse in her sink.*

When she lies back down, it occurs to Helen that her son had initially wanted a mouse. Of course! That's why they were in the small pet section looking at toys. His dream had been to look after a mouse. But working such long shifts in those days, the worry was that if David didn't look after it, the burden would fall on her. After coming in the door every night and making dinner, all Helen could do was collapse in front of the telly. Fish were a doddle, the shopkeeper assured them, much easier than rodents. Just sprinkle flakes through the hatch and wash out the tank when it turns green.

Helen gets out of bed. Goes to the window.

The curtains are milk white.

Each house on Westminster Crescent is glowing in its own way.

It was a mouse David really wanted, and in his mind had already begun to love.

Where was that love now?

Helen tries to understand what's happening to her, but each thought leads her back to the kitchen sink, where a lost wish has been granted.

And judging from the coloured toys still out on the patio, the mouse's willingness to take nuts, and its habit of staring, Helen is certain now that the creature in her sink must surely have been a child's pet that outlived his use as a companion and was left to die.

Except he is downstairs in a pie box. Not dying.

And for the first time in many years, against her better judgement, neither is she.

TUESDAY

17.

HELEN WAKES WITH a feeling of lightness, as though her dreams have carted away things long stored up. She dresses quickly and goes downstairs. Schumann is on the radio, his Lieder, and the mouse is asleep in his box.

Holding a cup of tea, Helen puts on her shoes and goes outside to look at the toys lying on the patio. It's cold, and she takes several deep breaths to clear any sleep. Each toy will have to be cleaned, of course, in the downstairs loo, then left on a towel in the hall to dry. If the creature is going to a wildlife centre—he should at least have his things.

Back inside, a sudden break in the music means news. It's a young man this time with a high voice. Bees are under threat. A small island near Japan is on fire. Children don't want milk anymore. In France, bus drivers are on strike while train drivers are threatening to strike over Christmas. And somebody in Cardiff has found a dinosaur skull in their back garden whilst illegally digging a kiddie pool.

According to the weather forecast, it's going to stay cold all day. Wind is pushing down from the north, while a thick band of low pressure could mean severe weather to come.

After finishing her tea Helen stands by the French door. Holds the mug with both hands because it's still warm. Everything outside is being whipped around by wind, lifted and then set back down.

She notices her tartan slippers in the corner, glued forever to the plastic boards. She will have to buy a new pair for winter. This mouse business is getting expensive. Still, he'll be off soon. Then she can lose herself in the old routine.

Helen makes another round of toast and sits on the couch flipping through the Yellow Pages. It's a few years out of date because everything is now on the computer.

Finally, Helen leafs to the correct section. There are two animal centres in the area. One is strictly for wildlife while the other takes in pets for people who can no longer care for them. It is obvious to her that calling the second place is the best idea. She doesn't want the creature to be gobbled up by some delirious fox, high on antibiotics. The thought that his small body could end up in something's jaws makes her shudder—and yet this is the world she had once been happy in.

When the extra ration of toast is finished, Helen returns to the hall. Turns down the radio. Dials the number.

"Pet Safe. Tony speaking."

"Ah, yes, hello. I'm calling because I recently found an abandoned pet."

There is a pause, then the person asks mockingly if it is really *her* pet that she doesn't want anymore.

"Of course it isn't," Helen snaps. "I just said it was abandoned."

"Do you know by who?"

"Is this Pet Safe or Pet Investigation?"

"Eh?"

"I've got an abandoned animal here in my house with nowhere to go."

"In your house?"

"That is correct. I found the creature in the street, brought him back, fed him, gave him water and a place to sleep, so he's stable."

"Sounds like you've made a friend."

"Well, I haven't."

"But you're caring for it. Can't the animal stay with you?"

"What you don't comprehend, Tony, is that I am an eighty-three-year-old woman who could die any second and then he'd be back to square one. Alone, vulnerable, and almost certainly malnourished."

"Dog or cat?"

"Smaller," Helen tells him.

"Rabbit, guinea pig, chinchilla, hamster, hedgehog, sugar glider . . ."

She can tell the man is reading off a list and it annoys her.

"It's a mouse."

"A mouse? Well, does it have a cage?"

"No, he's living in my sink."

"In your sink?"

"I needed a place where the thing couldn't escape."

"And you found it abandoned in the street?"

"Exactly."

"How did you get it back to your house if it doesn't have a cage?"

"It was living in a broken fish tank, which I carried home without realising there was a creature inside."

There is a brief pause while the man chuckles. "Not bad for somebody who could die at any second. Sounds to me like a wild mouse has made a nest in an old aquarium."

"Technically, I suppose, that could be true."

"Well, we only take in homeless pets."

"But this is a former pet mouse. I know because there was paraphernalia in the aquarium with it."

"Drugs?"

"Toys! A spinning wheel, a tube, a blue castle . . ."

"Oh, I thought you said *paraphernalia*."

Helen holds the phone at a distance from her head and shakes it violently.

"What I'm thinking has happened . . ." Tony goes on, making a nasal sound to imply deep thought, "is that somebody's hamster died, then after they put everything out for refuse collection, a wild mouse comes along, smells leftover rodent food, climbs in, and makes a nice home for itself."

Helen closes her eyes. "Are you a volunteer, Tony?"

"Yes, I am."

"Can I speak to a paid member of staff?"

"Everyone here is a volunteer. You should call wildlife rescue if you want someone from the council."

"Can you collect the mouse in my sink or can't you?"

"If you can prove to me he's a pet, our drop-off hours are ten to six, every day."

"But how am I supposed to prove that?"

"I don't know. I'm not a mouse expert."

"No," Helen says, "it doesn't sound like you're an expert at anything except being an idiot."

18.

FOR LUNCH, HELEN makes soup from a packet. The kind with croutons and green bits. *The mouse is still not awake, perhaps worn out*, Helen thinks, *from the many days of uncertainty leading up to his arrival in my sink.* She wonders if he considers her a mouse deity, and the pie box, lemonade cap, strawberries, and unsalted nuts part of a rodent's eternal reward.

After everything has been cleared from her meal, Helen notices it is almost noon. Half of Tuesday gone, just like that. She walks into the hall and turns off the radio, making sure not to step on the drying toys. In the sitting room she flops onto the couch and clicks on the telly. Still clutching the remote, she lets her eyes close.

When she opens them again, a film is starting. This wasn't in the *Radio Times*. Or perhaps she read the wrong column. Helen can't tell how long she has been asleep, but films on BBC Two usually begin at one fifteen. The opening music must have woken her. It is a picture Helen has not seen in a long time, but a film she knows well enough to recite all the most famous lines by her favourite character, the Tin Man.

A few scenes into the movie, Helen bolts to the kitchen and begins frantically searching for a container of some sort. The sight of her slippers gives her an idea. At first she tries simply pulling off a glue trap, but it is literally cemented, so she takes a pair of scissors and cuts around until there is no exposed glue, just a tartan slipper with a plastic sole.

She carries the slipper to the sink. There is no movement from the box but she knows the creature is inside. Time is running out. She fishes hurriedly for an unsalted nut from the packet beside the bread bin and waves it over the hole. Nothing. She taps the box gently with a nut. Helen can hear the film and knows the best song is about to come on. A grey head appears, its two eyes half-open and squinty. Helen drops the nut into the heel, then holds the slipper against the pie box. The mouse sniffs. Scratches his ear.

"C'mon, get in. There's something I want you to hear," she tells him, tossing a pinch of oats into the slipper. The mouse leaps in after them and Helen races into the sitting room. She can't believe she's doing this. What does she hope to achieve? It's the deep sea diver all over again. And what if the animal skedaddles? Starts running amok? There's no time to think about that. Back on the couch, she puts the slipper next to her leg on a cushion. The mouse is holding the nut in its paws like a small balloon. Then the song comes on. The one she learned by heart as a child when her father was at sea.

Helen is breathless. "That little girl is Judy Garland."

The mouse is now in the toe of the slipper, a bulge in the tartan fabric.

"I don't expect you to watch the film," she says to the end of its tail, "but do listen. It's a nice song about a rainbow . . . it's not really about that, you understand, it's about something else. I used to sing it when I was little, hoping that my father . . . wherever he was . . . might hear my voice and come home."

The tail moves, but the animal stays hidden.

"I know you can hear it because mice are expert listeners."

Once Dorothy has finished and is talking to her dog, Helen glances down at the slipper. "Why don't you come out and meet Toto." She remembers something then. Such a long time ago, but the feeling has not changed and comes to her in one piece.

"Once . . . " she explains, "during an air raid on the town, which had lots of factories back then, we were crammed into the basement of a brewery, surrounded by barrels of ale . . . and probably a few of your kind, I wouldn't doubt. I wasn't scared of the bombing, but other children were crying because their pets had been left behind. It made me so mad that I began to sing 'Over the Rainbow.' Do you know, after a verse or two, everyone joined in. We sang and sang until the all clear came. Then we left that place, not realising it was somewhere special that we would return to, over the years, in our minds.

"When we got outside, the sky blazed with fires. Everything burned and the air stung our eyes. In places, my mother and I had to walk with sleeves held against our noses and mouths. Some streets were just loose piles, but when we got closer we could see things in the bricks, like chairs or bits of piano, clothes . . . and, of course, other things . . . things that didn't look at all like when they were alive. But from the way my mother held my hand, I believed that nothing terrible would happen to us."

Helen taps the toe of the slipper with one finger and a grey head pops out.

"A few years after the war I fell into a big hole. What do you think of that? I sang the song then, too. It's why I rushed to get you from the sink, so you'd have the memory of it in case you end up somewhere like that."

An hour later, while anyone watching BBC Two is discovering the truth about the so-called wizard, the mouse waltzes boldly into the heel part of the slipper and stands up on his back legs—as if at the helm of a gondola.

Helen feels her breath quicken. "I thought mice were supposed to be scared of everything."

The animal sniffs. Its paws are clasped under his chin. The fur on his stomach is as soft as child's hair.

"If you're after more nuts, I think you've had enough. I'd like to eat Bakewell tarts all day but then where would we be?"

When the film ends, Helen watches the credits. Stares at the list of names without knowing a single thing about the people they once belonged to. She turns to the mouse, sitting quietly beside her in the slipper, as if watching television.

"The only consolation of being the last to go," she admits, "is knowing the people you loved the most won't suffer the way you do in their absence."

She leans back into a cushion. Folds her arms. There's no doubt in her mind now that he'll be safer at the shelter. It's not what she wants, but what she must do.

19.

AT DINNERTIME, HELEN carries the slipper back to the sink. When she sets it down the animal comes out and goes slowly to the bottle cap, making ripples as it drinks. She imagines the rain-sized drops sluicing its throat and entering the tiny stomach. After picking up a morsel of food in its path, the creature skips to his pie box without looking up.

Helen takes breaded fish pieces from the freezer. Washes a parsnip. Slices it down the middle with her sharpest knife. Arranges the pieces on a baking tray with the fish.

When everything is in, she imagines Tony from the animal shelter coming into her house with thick rubber gloves, a metal cage, and overalls that stink of bleach. He would have long hair and a stupid face. At some point she will have to call him back, apologize, and make the necessary arrangements.

Outside, the sky has turned. All through the house, shadows are opening like small umbrellas.

Before plating her meal, Helen collects the toys from the towel on the hall carpet and puts them in the sink. It's like setting up a miniature circus. She wonders if animal centres allow such personal items to be brought in, or are mice just plonked in a cage with other small rodents, who would almost certainly be less well behaved.

While she is smearing margarine on a parsnip, the mouse comes out. Goes quickly to the wheel. Sniffs. Climbs on as his little body sways with the sudden motion. Helen worries the creature might be startled, but a moment later he's running like mad with his tail in the air.

"You enjoy yourself while I eat my supper in the other room, then we'll both have strawberries for dessert. How does that sound?"

The mouse stops. Scratches his ear with a back foot.

Helen picks up her tray. "I'm Helen Cartwright. At least that's what people used to call me. And I wasn't always like this. You've caught me at a bad time."

The mouse leaps onto the high platform of his blue castle and begins waving his front paws as if signalling for help.

"I'll never know your name. But suppose I could give you one for the time we have left."

The mouse plops down to the sink and rushes to the lemonade cap. Dips his head for a sip's worth.

Helen watches. "That's it. I'll call you Sipsworth. It's old-fashioned like me."

WEDNESDAY

20.

HELEN SLEEPS DEEPLY and for much longer than usual. There are no dreams to remember, and the next day arrives in a pool of sun. When she turns to get out of bed, her feet instinctively search for slippers but find only thin carpet, warmed in patches where light has spilled through the curtains.

She pads downstairs and puts the radio on (Mozart). Sipsworth is awake, and when he sees Helen enter the kitchen, he hops onto his blue castle. All around him are tiny pills of fecal matter like miniature burnt sausages.

"You're looking for your breakfast, I expect."

She refills the lemonade cap in the downstairs loo, then pinches oats from the baking tin. She wants toast herself, and makes it while the kettle rises to a boil.

As Helen is scratching a film of margarine across each slice, the "March" from *Idomeneo* comes to an end. A woman's voice reads out the news. A small boat of refugees has sunk off the Spanish coast. The government has reached an impasse on education reform for secondary-aged children. England is through to the next round of the European Cup after beating Italy five goals to one. A mysterious disease has decimated the frog population of Sri Lanka. Petrol prices are up after going down.

Helen turns to the sink. Sips her tea.

"Those poor people in the boat," she says, imagining the chaos of arms and legs, then nothing but the white froth of lapping waves. "My father was shipwrecked. That was before your time. When I was a little girl."

She looks out the kitchen window into her wild garden. "If it wasn't for a life jacket, he wouldn't have had the strength to stay afloat, given the gash in his hip. Hopefully you'll never be lost at sea. But if you are, Sipsworth, maybe you'll get lucky like my father, and some nice fishermen will scoop *you* up."

The mouse is on his pie box with a disc of oat.

Helen turns to him. "Sometimes I marvel at how any of us get born at all. Not that I believe in a purpose, but something is going on."

Sipsworth turns the oat in his paws, as if waiting to eat until she's stopped talking.

After the national headlines, it is time for local news. Planning permission has been approved for the addition of a ring road—despite local protests about how the noise and pollution will affect cows that graze on the embankment overlooking the future dual carriageway. A spate of daylight burglaries has town residents on edge. Police are advising people to remain vigilant, and to keep doors and windows locked. Severe weather is expected overnight with high winds and the possibility of flooding. All nonessential travel should be postponed.

Helen takes her empty plate and rinses off crumbs in the downstairs loo. The linoleum floor is cool and damp on her bare feet.

"I'm going out today," she calls back to the kitchen. "Shopping. If there's anything you want . . ."

She rips a few squares of toilet paper from the roll, tearing them into smaller pieces when she reaches the kitchen sink. They flutter onto the pie box. Helen can hear him in there doing mouse chores and getting ready for bed.

When the kitchen is tidy, she tiptoes into the hall and dials the number for the pet shelter again. But this time it's an answer machine. She leaves a message along with her number, reminding Tony that she is *in extremis* and in no position to be hosting pets—or ferrying them to shelters in taxis.

On her way out, Helen closes the front door gently, so the slap of the letterbox won't wake him.

21.

PASSING THE PUBLIC library on her way to town, Helen has an idea. It is a drab, concrete structure with a flat roof and dark patches of lingering damp. But inside, the library is bright with the low sizzle of fluorescent bulbs.

As Helen approaches the counter, a kind face, older than hers, looks up.

"Good morning. Are we new to the area?"

Helen shakes her head. "Not at all. I've just never been in."

The librarian lays a form and a short orange pencil on the counter. Pushes them toward Helen with both hands. "For your library card."

Helen looks at them. "Before we get to any of that I'd like to know if you even have the books I'm interested in."

The old librarian's expression changes, more confusion than annoyance.

"Only members can check out books. But have no fear . . ." she says, tapping the form, "it's all free."

Helen sighs. "Fine, but while I'm doing it, would you look up some titles for me please? The subject being *mice*."

"Mice?"

"Exactly. Please search for any books with *mice* or *mouse* in the title."

The old woman squints at the computer. Helen picks up the pencil and fills out a few boxes to show that she, too, is doing her bit.

"Oh, you're in luck!" cries the librarian, putting on her glasses to search the aisle behind Helen. "Dominic!"

Helen turns to see a little man in his forties pushing a cart. He has on a T-shirt with all the planets and their distance in miles from the sun.

"Dominic . . . can you spare a moment?"

The man mumbles something, then walks stiffly to the counter and stares at Helen without blinking.

"Hello, Dominic," Helen says.

"Okay," he replies, looking around.

The librarian rips a sheet of paper from the printer and hands it to him. "Dominic helps us keep everything in order, don't you, Dominic?"

Dominic shrugs.

His belly has enlarged the planet Pluto to many times its actual size.

"Once you've finished filling out the card, Dominic will be back with your books. Won't you, Dominic?"

Helen has no choice now. She is going to have to become a member of the town library. The librarian takes the completed form, and with surgical precision enters Helen's data into the computer using the one-finger technique.

× × ×

Fifteen minutes later it's done, and a machine spits out a plastic card with Helen's name, address, and a barcode for the library's new self-checkout system.

Dominic has returned. He is pushing the cart and groaning.

"Don't worry," the librarian whispers. "He always does that . . . it's part of his condition."

The librarian comes around the counter and inspects the books on Dominic's cart. "Take as many as you can manage, Mrs. Cartwright."

Helen inspects the many volumes, but most are large and flat with colourful drawings of mice wearing clothes or driving cars.

"These are children's books," she says. "I'm looking for books about real mice."

"Oh, I see. Nonfiction! You should have said. But look here . . ." The librarian slides out a small paperback and reads the title aloud. "*Mice: A Complete Pet Owner's Manual* by Sharon L. Vanderlip, with a Special Chapter on Understanding Your Mouse."

Dominic tiptoes up for a closer look. "What's your mouse's name? Or do you just call it Mouse?"

"Who said I have a mouse?"

Dominic touches the tips of his fingers together. Looks at the orange library carpet.

"Well, since you ask, Dominic, it's Sipsworth."

"Lovely!" exclaims the librarian. "Isn't that something? What a wonderful book you've found for Mrs. Cartwright and her mouse."

Helen coughs. "He's not my mouse. I'm just looking after him until suitable arrangements can be made."

The librarian touches her lacquered bead necklace. "Then I'm sure you'll find this book very useful."

Before Helen leaves, the librarian forces a piece of fluorescent green paper into her hand.

"We have coffee hour once a week. I'll be there along with a few other patrons, so at least you'll know one person."

"It's boring," Dominic says, a little more relaxed now. He points to the librarian. "Usually just me and Mum. But there is cake."

22.

When Helen is safely around the corner, she drops the flyer into a wastepaper basket then checks for the bulge of the mouse book in her handbag.

Life gathers pace once she reaches the shopping arcade. As the lift always smells of urine, Helen heads for the stairs, past a row of benches where strangers sit, side by side, watching others like them with canes, missing teeth, hats, old-fashioned hair, and names that no longer possess any more significance than words on a bus pass.

After purchasing a new pair of rubber-soled tartan slippers at Marks, Helen buys coffee at one of the more expensive places, paying a few pence extra to sit in the café itself.

She would normally have resisted the temptation of a cake or tart from the display case—but as the morning has gone so well, Helen points to a chocolate-dipped macaroon. She's had enough interaction with people for one day, and sits several tables away from anyone else.

Helen takes out the book and flicks to the section on food. Her instincts were correct. Raw seeds, nuts, and grains combined with fresh fruits and vegetables will "keep mealtimes interesting." There is also special mouse food that can be purchased at pet shops. Anything salted, cooked, processed, or containing caffeine or chocolate is usually harmful. On each page of her book is a paw containing some tip or fact about mice. The paw on page forty-five advises caregivers that mice sometimes practice coprophagy, whereby eating their own feces allows them to "synthesize their own vitamin C and efficiently recover many B vitamins also." Reading this reminds Helen of the life she had in Australia. The one that seemed always beyond the reaches of change but is now a single person away from extinction.

On her walk back, dark clouds are gathering like witches' cloaks over the town. When Helen is almost at the sign that says WESTMINSTER CRESCENT, a fierce hand of wind parts the limbs of a horse chestnut, thrashing the branches.

"I'm home," she calls, stepping inside and closing the mustard door behind her. "The weather forecast was right for once. I think we're in for a night of it."

The house is warm and quiet. Helen puts her key on the hall table beside the radio. "You may be interested to know I have raw, unsalted, organic cashews. I've had my treat already, while I was out. And we're members of the library now . . . though most of the books they have about your kind are mercilessly archetypal."

Helen stares at the phone and wonders if Tony from the wildlife centre has called. She doesn't have an answer machine, so lifts the handle to listen for the drone of a dial tone.

In the kitchen Helen cuts the plastic tags off her new slippers. The mouse is asleep, so instead of boiling the kettle, she fills a glass in the downstairs loo and drinks it in the hall.

Although it is only late afternoon, Helen puts all the downstairs lights on. When the foul weather really digs in, she should probably close the curtains, then she and the mouse can huddle on the couch in their slippers.

With her feet tucked under a cushion, Helen reads a section from her book called "The Body Language of Your Mouse."

"*Your* . . ." Helen says aloud. "Sounds funny, as though he's a material commodity."

But then she understands it means *your* as in *your responsibility*.

When her eyes need a rest from the page, she turns on the television. It is still children's programmes, but soon the Australian soaps will start, then the news, then evening dramas, talk shows, or perhaps a film, "though please god not something from America," Helen grumbles, "all sex, guns, money, and drug taking." Not like the crackling pictures before the war, she recalls, with gentle men in tails and women in silver gowns with high, soft shoes.

Helen gets up. Goes over to the French door. Everything in her garden is being tossed about as strings of rain lash the glass.

"It'll be back into the ark before long," she mouths to her reflection.

In the kitchen, Sipsworth is standing on his pie box licking a paw, oblivious to any drama beyond the sink.

"Grooming," Helen says. "That's what you're doing, according to the book." She knows now not to move quickly, as freshly woken mice can become moody if startled.

She holds out the slipper. "C'mon. There's a cartoon on the telly you should see. Make the most of it because they might not have televisions in the shelter."

When the six o'clock news comes on, it's time to cook supper. Helen carries Sipsworth in the slipper back to the kitchen and sets him on the counter beside the bread bin. From the cupboard she takes a packet of instant mashed potato and a can of beans. She thinks it might be nice to have a cheese and onion slice, but doesn't feel like cooking it from frozen.

"This'll have to do. I'm not that hungry anyway."

Helen boils the kettle. Pours hot water into the bowl of potato flakes. By the time they've fluffed up, the beans are bubbling on the stove. She plates everything. Takes out the small chopping board. Then a knife. Prepares a fruit and nut salad for the mouse's supper.

Sipsworth is still on the counter in his slipper, but with both front paws resting on the back heel, as though at any moment he might spring out. This frightens Helen. What if he runs under the knife and is decapitated? Or touches a paw to the kettle?

Helen carries the slipper to the sink and Sipsworth hops onto the pie box as though it is something they have rehearsed. It's raining so hard Helen can hear it on the roof of their home like a shower of coins.

When the mouse's meal is ready, Helen impulsively holds out a fragment of cashew, Sipsworth grabs onto her finger and pulls himself into her palm.

Helen doesn't know what to do, but is afraid to move in case her sudden action hurts him. The house is now creaking like old timber, and outside in the street, she can hear glass breaking.

Helen notices her hand trembling—not because she's holding a live mouse, but because it's the first time she's been touched by another living thing for over twenty years.

And then the lights go out.

"Bugger," says an old voice in the darkness.

23.

SIPSWORTH SHUFFLES A little, but the small weight is steady in her hand.

"Don't move and don't be afraid. It's just a power cut." Helen knows she can't stay on her feet and steps gingerly to the sitting room, feeling for the doorframe with one hand. She locates the couch by moving up against it, then slowly sits, resting her occupied hand on a cushion. Helen feels him move then, from her palm onto her thigh, where he stretches his body out. After some minutes she realises her mouse is sleeping. She is sure because the shallow bite of his claws has released her skirt.

"For god's sake stay there," she whispers, "or we'll lose each other."

Her sight swims through the darkness, searching for something familiar, some shadow to use as a ledge.

"I was once stuck in a well. Did I tell you that? It was darker than this and I was alone. It happened at the beginning of my life. In the end an animal saved me. A dog. When they got me out and were undoing the rope, my father was on his knees crying. I think that frightened me more than being in the well. I remember the strength in my mother's arms when she lifted me up. You remind me of them, Sipsworth . . . the way you go about your own business with quiet cheerfulness. Definitely a Cartwright."

"There's no one alive who'd remember this . . . but did I tell you that Len took my last name when we were married? That's right. This is not something he liked to talk about, but as a baby he was left on a doorstep. The police came and he was taken to a home for boys where social services gave him the name Leonard Dunedin after the people whose doorstep he was left on, Mr. and Mrs. Leonard of Dunedin Drive. Bit daft if you ask me, Sipsworth. And Len never liked it, so when we were married he felt that Cartwright was closer to who he was, and would I mind . . . well of course I didn't. And even though he met Mum and Dad only a handful of times, he was like a son to them. Oh, Sipsworth, they were such lovely people. There's so much I wish I could say to them, not as my parents . . . but as people who shared their lives with me."

Helen has never sat like this in darkness before, at least without the telly on. Outside, bins are blowing up the middle of Westminster Crescent with their lids thumping.

"Apart from family, Len's great passion was trains, toy engines that is. I always knew what to buy him for Christmas. David was more into model cars. I don't suppose you've ever ridden on a train, Sipsworth. These days they're very fast, the real ones I mean . . . but back then there were dining cars with candles and real cutlery. My first time in a proper one . . . going to Edinburgh . . . I was very nervous, and made sure to keep my elbows off the table and to push my food on the back of the fork, the way they do it in old films. I was so worried about spilling my soup . . . but in the end it wasn't even on the menu . . . it was . . . Galia melon. Then something hot with gravy. When the time came for dessert, it was freezing cold in the car because the porter had all windows open to let out the smoke from people's cigarettes. My mother was wearing a fur coat, almost the same colour as yours, Sipsworth, and she wrapped it around the both of us. All I could smell then was perfume. And the sound of my parents' voices must have lulled me to sleep, for when I woke up it was bagpipes! Someone was playing on the railway station platform to honour the servicemen and -women getting off the train. 'Flowers of the Forest' my father said the song was. There was a lot of that back then, because it helped people . . . it reassured them that anyone they'd lost was being acknowledged from every corner of Britain."

Helen rolls into another memory, and then another, as darkness smudges the boundaries of past and present.

When she feels sleep pushing like an enormous flower trying to open, Helen scoops the sleeping mouse off her leg and carries him in her palm to the kitchen. His body is warm and soft, the weight of two fingers. Her eyes have adjusted, and in the breath of a rising moon, she can now discern the outlines of objects she knows.

Once over the sink, Helen lowers her hand to the pie box. The mouse doesn't move.

"C'mon now, it's time for bed."

His claws dig in like tiny pads of Velcro.

"I don't care if you're nocturnal. You can't come upstairs, I'm afraid you might get stuck in some nook or cranny you can't get out of, like I did in that well."

Helen uses her free hand to nudge his body, but the mouse is holding fast.

"You *must* go to bed," she tells him, quietly. "It's just rain now, there's really nothing to be afraid of."

She knows he doesn't understand and turns her hand slowly over the cardboard hole, so he'll soon be upside down.

A moment before tipping, the mouse drops down. Even though Helen can't see him, she hears his small feet and can sense his disappointment.

Her dinner is still on the plate, but cold now. She'll go to bed without anything, and make a fresh start in the morning. She reaches for the fruit and nut mix, sprinkles some around the sink, then feels her way to the stairs.

Without brushing her teeth or her hair, Helen sheds her clothes and gets into bed. The sheets are so cold they could be wet. She moves a pillow so it sits beneath her knees. Then she is quite still.

Blinking her eyes, Helen goes over the things that have happened that day. Replays conversations in the library with Dominic and his mother. Wonders where they are . . . and *if* they are awake, what thoughts and memories are rowing them out to the deep waters of sleep.

THURSDAY

24.

AT DAWN HELEN wakes to the flutter of voices. Sits on the side of her bed not fully awake. Are they people she knew? British accents or Australian? She can't decide, but shuffles into her new slippers. Then on the top step she realises it's just the power come back.

Downstairs, she turns off all the lights and the television. Flicks on the radio. It's the Finnish Baroque Orchestra, live from Wigmore Hall.

The mouse is sleeping, but spread around the sink, evidence of nocturnal prancing in the form of tiny cigars. Helen picks them up one by one with a piece of kitchen towel. She isn't squeamish about flesh or blood or feces. Never was.

Finally, with a tray of tea and toast on the coffee table, she gets comfortable on the couch with her book on mice, specifically page thirty-nine, "Housing Considerations." He simply can't go on living in the sink—even for the short time he is to remain with her on Westminster Crescent. The fish tank on the patio has a crack in it, and though Helen considers putting tape over the line, fragments of glass might lodge in his paw. Such small pieces would be impossible to remove, even for a skilled surgeon with a magnifying glass.

Helen also reads the section on “Secondary Enclosures,” but there’s nothing relevant to her as a foster parent. If she could find *another* fish tank, that would be fine. But where she placed it in the house would be of equal importance to the dimensions. No drafts, no direct sunlight, no dust, and no sudden changes in humidity or temperature, according to the book. When the air reaches 37 degrees centigrade, a mouse begins to die.

After breakfast, Helen realises she’s missed the news and weather. The radio is on but she was engrossed in her library book. Most interesting to her is the section on mouse moods, specifically their unwillingness to bite anything that isn’t food, and how sudden noises can lead to unexpected loss of heart function. Such timid creatures.

After half an hour, Helen gets up. Goes into the kitchen. Stands over the box. Has an idea. Swaps her tartan slippers for shoes and pulls on a coat over her cardigan. Gets ready to go out. She can’t believe it herself. Soon she’ll be running marathons.

Before leaving the house, she lifts the phone and dials the number of the animal shelter again. But it rings and rings without giving her the chance to leave another message.

With a sense of heaviness she can’t ascribe to anything in particular, Helen buttons her coat. After checking for the key, she steps out—gripping the tongue of the letterbox as she pulls the front door slowly and shuts it with a low click.

She hasn’t brought any bags because she does not intend to carry her purchase home. It’s not raining but everything is soggy from last night's storm. How it pains her to take the hill into town two days in a row—but what a relief it will be to use the sink again.

Outside the air is crisp and the sky so blue it seems painted. Large puddles wear patches of fallen leaves.

Helen crests the hill.

Passes the school, then the library.

Outside the Butcher's Arms, two plant pots lie on their sides. One is intact, while the other is cracked, spilling soil like grainy blood across the pavement. A grey drainpipe sags over Tudor windows. Farther down the street, a tree is down. Despite the carnage, town is quiet but for shopkeepers standing in small groups, pointing to things on or near their premises.

When Helen finally reaches her destination, she finds the door held open by a rubber wedge. She approaches the counter and sees the owner typing something into his till.

Helen undoes the buttons on her overcoat. "It's very hot in here."

"That'll be the space heaters, madam. I have to test them, as once or twice they've been damaged on the boat. I hope you're not after brooms and bin bags because I've sold out. Everyone and their uncle has been in since I opened at eight o'clock. What a storm we had!"

"I need a fish tank," Helen announces. "A rather large one."

"Now that's what I call an intelligent hobby. Salt or fresh?"

"I beg your pardon?"

"Is it tropical fish or goldfish, madam?"

"Nothing like that . . . I want it for something else."

The man comes toward her from behind the counter. "May I ask what it's for if not aquatics? My guess would be some sort of experimental gardening. You seem the type."

Before Helen can answer, the man's face opens. "You were in here before looking for glue traps!" A meaty hand is extended. "Nice to see you back. I'm Cecil Parks," he says. "So, did you have any luck with the little bugger?"

Helen feels blood spread into her cheeks.

"Did you catch anything, missus?"

"I did, actually, yes."

"They're quite effective, aren't they? Though the mouse is often captured alive, which is unfortunate."

"It's more than unfortunate, Mr. Parks . . . it's criminal. Those glue *things* should be illegal."

Cecil clears his throat. "To be honest, missus, the fate of mice is not something I've given serious thought to . . ."

He is interrupted then by the squelch of wet shoes. Someone entering the shop.

"Can I help you, sonny?" Cecil calls brusquely.

"No, just looking, cheers," says a young voice.

Cecil scowls at the boy, who is rattling something on a shelf behind Helen.

"Sorry, missus . . . you were saying?"

"Yes, Mr. Parks, mice are capable of great feeling and so I'm surprised that a man of your good moral sense and sensitivity would sell such barbaric items as glue traps." She pauses to see his reaction and can tell his feelings are hurt. "Experience has taught me, Cecil," Helen goes on gently, "that the only decent thing to do might be to sell the type of device where you trap the creature alive, then let it go in its natural habitat."

Before he can say anything, the other customer moves to a different aisle.

"Excuse me," Cecil says, following the squelch of the boy's wet shoes.

A moment later the shopkeeper is back. "He's gone. Up to no good if you ask me. Now, as for all this mouse business, if I do as you ask, can you kindly tell me what I'm supposed to say to my customers when they come in looking for mousetraps because rodents are eating them out of house and home, or toileting where food is prepared?"

"You are the final authority on hardware in this town, Mr. Parks, and if you explain how humane traps work, people will listen."

"They're expensive . . ."

"Not in the long run . . ." Helen is thinking on her feet, "because unlike glue and snap traps—this type of thing can be reused."

Cecil taps his chin with the tops of both fingers. "But what am I going to do with all the wall space?"

"Fill it with fish things! An 'intelligent hobby,' you called it."

The big shopkeeper folds his arms. Smiles at the old woman standing before him. "Cecil's Aquatic Supply Centre," he says, reading words on an imaginary sign. "Food, filters, fish, and fine habitats. What do you think?"

Helen closes her eyes. "Lovely!"

"Really?"

"Oh, yes, and think of the revenue you'll generate as more people enter the hobby."

"I think we might be onto something there, missus . . ."

"Cartwright . . . Helen Cartwright."

Cecil takes a step back. "Cartwright? Not the teacher's daughter who went to Australia?"

Helen has not expected this and although her lips move, they do not form any words.

"Your father taught me to read, Mrs. Cartwright! It was very hard, *very* hard at first, but every day after school I stayed on for an hour with your father. Six months it took! Most people would have given up. That would have been . . . oh . . . let me see . . . 1986 . . . yes because Maradona did that handball thing in the World Cup."

"My father retired that year."

The shopkeeper grins. "Not because of me I hope."

"He was made to, Mr. Parks, it was mandatory in those days when you reached a certain age. I'd been in Australia almost thirty years by then.

He whistles. "Thirty years . . . your father talked about you no end! And to think, here you are now, standing in my shop, asking me to consider the fate of mice!"

Helen's left arm goes numb. She blinks rapidly as dizziness liquefies the room.

"You've gone a bit pale, Mrs. Cartwright. Come in the back and have a cup of tea."

"I can't," she groans, trying to make a fist. "You have customers . . ."

"There's no one here now but us. Let's go in the back and sit down."

Cecil leads Helen to the back of the shop, where he takes her coat and puts her handbag on a small table. There are unopened boxes and Christmas decorations piled on top, and a stack of Advent calendars in cellophane. The man fills a silver kettle from the cold tap and plugs it in.

"I've been meaning to hire someone, but can't find the right person . . . now, there are biscuits somewhere . . ."

"Oh, don't trouble yourself on my account, please . . . I'll be fine in a minute."

"Not only did he teach me to read, Mrs. Cartwright, but your father used to give me sandwiches, which your mother walked up to the school so they were fresh."

Helen imagines her aging mother at the counter in her chequered apron, cutting the crusts off bread. "Let me guess, Cecil. Fish paste? Cheese and pickle?"

"That's it! My own father lived apart from the family, up in Lancashire, and my mother worked long hours at the distillery making bottles. But that's all been closed down for yonks."

Helen is starting to feel herself again. "We hid there from the bombs during the war."

"So I heard. Them cellars went all the way down to the devil himself. The whole thing is a truck stop now, with an all-night restaurant and a dozen petrol pumps . . . they even have showers for the drivers and a truck wash."

When the kettle's boiled, Cecil opens a small tin and digs with his fingers.

"Bags okay? I don't bother with the pot since it's just me, though it certainly makes for a better cup."

While the tea is brewed, the shopkeeper slips bourbons, custard creams, and a few digestives onto a chipped plate.

"This'll perk us both up, I fancy."

Helen drinks her tea without speaking. The last time she was seated so close to somebody was on the flight to London over three years ago.

Cecil snaps a biscuit. "I remember your father like it was yesterday. Polished shoes and a faint floral smell . . . like sandalwood."

Helen sets her cup down. "Astor. That was the name of his aftershave. I'm not even sure they make it anymore. Do you have children, Cecil?"

"No, Mrs. Cartwright, I can't say I do. I did have someone, a partner. But . . . you know."

"No, tell me, Cecil."

"They went to Spain."

"They?"

"Well . . . he went to Spain, I should say. Ibiza. To live."

Helen locks Cecil in a stare. "How terrible."

"Oh right, yes, well it knocked me for six, I can tell you. I'm used to it now, of course, though am ashamed to admit I've looked for him on the internet, and can't find a thing. Not a sausage."

Helen lifts the plate to offer Cecil one of his own biscuits. "It obviously wasn't meant to be."

"You think so, Mrs. Cartwright?"

"Of course. Otherwise it would be, wouldn't it?"

Cecil chuckles. "I suppose that's true. I used to have quite long hair, and it was just after I'd had it cut. I always wonder what would have happened if I hadn't gone to the hairdresser that day. If things would be different."

"Oh Cecil, people don't leave each other because of haircuts. It was probably something personal to him, a reason that you'll never know."

Cecil searches the corners of the room with his eyes, as if looking for the reason that has eluded him these past seventeen years.

"Well, you've got a good business here. My father would have been proud of everything you've done."

"Do you think so?"

"He never would have spent so much time with you if he hadn't seen great promise."

Cecil squeezes more custard creams onto the biscuit plate.

"I'm big into lawn bowls now, Mrs. Cartwright. And last year was elected treasurer of the District Bowls Club. Not bad for a boy who couldn't read until he was thirteen."

Helen nods approvingly then crunches on a stale biscuit.

"Our green has seven rinks, Mrs. Cartwright. Seven!"

"Is that a lot?"

"Let's just say it's the biggest lawn bowling establishment north of Oxford and south of Northampton. We were founded in 1921. You should come and spectate on Saturday. There's a tea room, a small selection of cakes, lovely club chairs, of course, and a complete library of bimonthly newsletters going back almost a century. We're currently running a membership drive for NHS doctors and nurses from the new Meadowpark Hospital. Lawn bowling is scientifically proven to reduce stress levels."

When the tea in her cup has cooled, Helen gets to her feet and smiles.

"If you'd show me what fish tanks you have, Cecil, I must be getting back."

"Well, I don't actually keep fish tanks in stock, but can order any size you like."

"Oh dear, and how long does that take?"

"I could ask them to rush it. Maybe a week? But last night's storm might slow things."

"I'm afraid it's rather urgent."

"You could try the pet shop in Banbury or go into Oxford tomorrow."

"I don't have a car, and couldn't possibly take it on the bus."

"Why not?"

"Because there are people on it!"

Cecil looks confused and then laughs. "That's a good one."

The shop floor is bright and empty.

"It's quite peaceful here, isn't it?" Helen says.

"Now it is, but sometimes I have a queue of ten people. I desperately need to find someone. The demand for hardware in this town has grown so much, I've started opening on Sundays."

"Sundays?"

"Well . . . everyone does it these days, don't they, Mrs. Cartwright?"

"You should put a notice in the window, if you need help. That's how it's done in Australia."

Cecil touches a finger to his lips. "What if I could get you the tank in three days?"

Helen imagines a van from the shelter pulling up outside. The faces of animals on the side and the back full of cages that stink of bleach and urine. "I most likely won't need it by then, Mr. Parks."

"Wait, I have an idea," he says, pulling a tatty notebook from his pocket. "I have to deliver a chain saw and rope to a village near Banbury, so technically I could go in on your behalf, buy the tank, then drop it off on my way back."

Helen bites her lip. It would mean someone coming into the house, which hasn't happened since she moved in. But then she would have the fish tank today.

"That would be very kind, Cecil. I'll have cash ready to reimburse you."

"A cheque works, too, Mrs. Cartwright. You ought to be careful keeping cash in the house with all these burglaries going on."

"Oh, I'm not worried about that . . . I've got nothing to steal."

Cecil takes a piece of paper and a pen from the counter. "Write down your address. Can I ask what the tank is for again?"

Helen hesitates. Chooses her words with care. "You'll see when you arrive. Something a bit unexpected."

25.

On her way home, Helen pops into the supermarket for lettuce, blueberries, and peas. Things listed in the mouse book as foods a mature male might enjoy. Passing through the refrigeration section Helen stops, as usual, to consider the packages of sausages. For a few horrible moments, she imagines Sipsworth's body, pink and raw, rolled onto a tray and covered with clear plastic. She looks around at the other shoppers.

How has she not seen this before?

A workman holding a can of Pepsi, a packet of crisps, and a hard hat is surveying a selection of processed meat products. *If mice are capable of giving and receiving love*, Helen reasons, *are not pigs, cows, and chickens of equal intelligence?*

Impulsively, she clears her throat to get the workman's attention, then shakes her head with a grimace. The man seems on the verge of laughing, but then understands the old woman is trying to warn him. He nods sagely, giving her a thumbs up as he backs away from the unknown menace of a pork pie; the mysterious terror of a Cornish pasty.

Helen imagines herself standing in the supermarket aisle with a sign, red-faced and glaring at anyone who dares pick up a meat product. The police would come and escort her to the exit. Down at the station they would bring her tea and reassure her that eating meat is natural for humans. We're built for it.

But Helen would argue.

Are not anger, jealousy, and lust natural by the very same logic? Is every action we're built for morally justifiable?

The truth does not fear authority! she remembers reading in a French novel. She could spray it on the windows of butchers' shops in the middle of the night.

Passing through an aisle with chocolate on one side and boiled sweets on the other, Helen continues the oratory in her mind.

Without meat, she expounds to the gathering faces, *no one would starve. Quite the contrary. More people could be fed. Therefore, eating meat is nothing more than a cruel entertainment.*

Descending the hill, Helen feels the sting of self-righteous anger ebb with the effort to get home. But once inside she goes straight for the freezer and takes out all the chicken pies. Stacks them quietly on the counter so as not to wake the mouse. The cupboard is next. At the back is a tin of corned beef, which she sets down with the frozen food.

Hovering over the sink, Helen leans toward the pie box, hoping for a glimpse of paw, or nose, or quick round of ear. Some flash of encouragement for what she's about to do.

"If I'm not prepared to eat you," she whispers to the hole, "then I have no moral basis for eating other animals."

When the corned beef and frozen pies are in a bag with all the other meat products from her kitchen, Helen takes a stainless steel serving spoon and tin opener from the drawer. Goes into the back garden. For the next hour, on her hands and knees, Helen digs a large hole. It's hard work at first, but the soil passing through her hands is satisfying. As she's laying the items to rest, Helen considers that what she's doing could be a sign of some mental condition connected to old age. But people can just bugger off. The only inconvenience for her is that vegetarians live longer, according to a BBC Two documentary she watched last week.

When the doorbell rings two hours later, Helen is fast asleep on the couch with the television going. A documentary on arable farming has just ended. She wakes to her name spoken through the letterbox. In the front hall, a smudge of white is visible through the frosted glass. When she opens the door, it's Cecil, and at his feet a new glass fish tank.

"When I called there was only one left, so I went early."

"You closed the shop, Cecil?"

"Well, let's just say I took a longer than normal lunch hour. Another reason why I'm going to need someone . . . we're fast becoming a delivery culture like America."

Helen stands to one side and Cecil carries the fish tank into the hall.

"Where do you want it?"

"On the kitchen counter . . . beside the bread bin. I've already made room."

Helen closes the door and follows behind his large frame. A moment after setting down the tank, Cecil notices a small head looking at him from a cardboard box in the sink.

"He's here as my guest, Cecil, so please don't say anything negative."

"How unusual. More curious than frightened. Looks like you've made him at home."

"Well, it's only temporary. There's only so long a woman of my age can fill her kettle from the downstairs loo."

As Cecil stands there, cup of tea in one hand, biscuit in the other, Helen wipes out the tank. Lines the bottom with toilet paper. One by one, she transfers the mouse's things from the sink into his new home. As he is not a shy mouse, Helen had expected him to be moving about, inhaling the aroma of someone new. But in the few days since their acquaintance, Helen has also noticed that Sipsworth is a deep sleeper.

"May I see the garden, Mrs. Cartwright?"

As she fiddles with the lock, Cecil says, "I can fix that if you want."

"I won't be here long enough to appreciate it, but thank you."

"Moving are you?"

Helen smiles. "Moving on you might say, once this mouse business is cleared up."

But the shopkeeper is distracted by the garden. "Don't suppose anything's been cut back for years. And here's me thinking you had green fingers, Mrs. Cartwright."

Where the patio stones end and lawn begins is a small pile of rubbish. An empty corned beef can and chicken pie boxes. Beside it, a hump of freshly dug earth.

Cecil nudges the empty can with his polished brogue shoe. "Looks like someone's been camping."

Helen clears her throat. "There's the old fish tank, with the crack," she points out. "That's how he got here. In the bottom of that, with all his things piled on top of him."

Cecil bends to inspect it. "If you want, I can carry it out for you. It's rubbish collection day tomorrow."

"Oh, it's not in my way, Cecil. I never come out here."

"But you should! It's a nice little garden. You might even think about growing some carrots and lettuce for his lordship in the sink."

"As I said, he's not staying. All this is temporary. I'm about to make arrangements with a shelter for collection. Don't animals want to be with their own kind?"

Cecil rubs his chin. "If ever I *was* an animal, I don't remember it."

"I see you as a beaver," Helen says impulsively. "Very industrious . . . always building."

When they go back inside, it's Cecil's turn to fiddle with the handle on the French door. "The cylinder's just about had it. And you really need a good lock these days with all the daylight burglaries."

Helen is already in the hall counting out notes for the fish tank. She walks Cecil to the door of his white van.

"If your father could see us now, Mrs. Cartwright . . . I think he'd be very happy."

Back inside, Helen has to stop in the downstairs loo to blow her nose. Dab the corners of both eyes. When she returns to the kitchen, Sipsworth is popping up and down on his pie box.

Helen looks down at him. "All this is your fault, you know. I hope you're proud of yourself."

26.

After a cheese sandwich and cup of sugary tea, Helen walks around the house, trying to decide where the fish tank should go. Based on what she has learned in the mouse book, it should be out of direct sunlight and away from drafts. Eventually it seems like the space in front of the couch will be best. It's shady, warm, and surrounded by soft things. The only drawback is that he will be next to her when she's watching television and trying to concentrate.

Helen moves slowly and carefully, but it's not as heavy as the damaged one she brought in almost a week ago. When the tank is in place with all his toys inside, she considers calling the animal shelter, but decides instead to have a quick rest. She drops onto the couch and pulls up her feet so they're under a cushion. Picks up the *Radio Times* to see what's on. Fairly soon her eyes want to close and she lets them.

× × ×

When Helen wakes, it's nearing dinnertime. Children's programmes are still on, and the television has cast a pleasant glow over the whole room. The new fish tank is on the floor with the mouse's things.

Helen gets up quickly and goes into the kitchen, wondering what to make. Peering into the cupboard, she hears movement in the sink. Sipsworth is out and drinking from his lemonade cap.

"There's no television tonight," she says. "Just radio, I'm afraid . . . an Italian opera playing live from Covent Garden."

She watches him study the various items of food lying about, then turns back to the cupboard. Outside, a gentle, soundless rain is rinsing the houses and gardens of Westminster Crescent.

Helen brings down a can of tomato soup and plugs in the toaster.

"Oh, Len hated opera," she says, opening the bread bin. "Thought it was just a bunch of hairy fellas in tights shouting at one another. But that's Australian men for you. Still, he took me every year to Sydney on my birthday, got dressed up, too. Sat through the entire thing without closing a single eye. After we lost him, there was an intermission of seven years . . . then my son started taking me."

The toast pops up. Helen pours the bubbling soup into a bowl.

"Though, we took the train, as my son didn't enjoy driving. Even when he was grown up he didn't want a car. 'You can't walk to school,' I said. David was a junior schoolteacher, did I mention that? 'No,' he told me, 'but I can walk to the bus stop, Mum.' Always an answer for everything."

"Of course, I'd saved his father's Jaguar, a silver XJS. Had it serviced every six months. A Greek man would come to us early from the garage and drive it away until evening. But David didn't want it. Wouldn't even sit in it. Preferred public transport to his own father's car."

Helen crunches her toast. For the second time this week, she's eating in the kitchen.

"I gave my son a hard time about that bloody car. It's like he didn't want to know his own father."

Helen rinses her bowl. Draws a glass of water and drinks without stopping.

Once the dishes and pot are upside down on a tea towel, Helen goes upstairs and has a long, hot bath. She's back in Australia, moving from scene to scene like someone on a set. "Wherever you are, David, I hope you can forgive your old mother for that car business."

She remembers the look on his face after she'd humiliated him for not caring. He had tried to be honest with his mother and she had berated him for it.

Helen wipes her eyes with a corner of towel. "My sweet David."

Then, as often happens in moments like this, she can hear her son's voice coming to her from somewhere far away, urging his mother to forgive herself.

Ten minutes before the opera begins, Helen rifles for something at the back of her wardrobe. A gold and green dress with cuffed sleeves, low neckline, and pleats at the skirt. It hasn't fit for a long time and in the bathroom mirror her body appears bony and shrunken, as though she were the survivor of an apocalypse.

When Helen enters the kitchen, Sipsworth leaps onto his pie box. Waves his paws the way children signal to low-flying aircraft.

"Don't laugh," she says. "It may look ridiculous to you, but this dress was once the height of fashion."

Helen fingers the fabric. The silk is like warm breath.

"Why I didn't throw it away for the big move, I'll never know."

She drinks another glass of water filled from the downstairs loo. Flicks the radio on. The orchestra is warming up, and the announcer giving a brief history of the Royal Opera House.

"C'mon, Sips . . ." she says, picking up the pie box. "I've got a surprise for you."

She carries it carefully, along with the lemonade cap of water. Once in the fish tank, he climbs out, smelling and touching everything with a left or right paw in case there's danger.

"It's like your old place, just dry and clean."

But after a few moments, he's bouncing on top of his blue castle, wanting to come out again.

"I have no idea what you're trying to say, but the sink is mine."

When the overture begins, Helen lowers his slipper and Sipsworth hops in. She puts it on the cushion next to her, and it's where he remains, quite contentedly, for most of the first act, with Helen going on about who's who and why everyone is laughing—or who the girl is that's been mistakenly kidnapped by the count's henchmen.

At intermission, Helen carries the slipper into the kitchen and makes a cup of tea. She fills the kettle from the downstairs loo as laughter flutters from her mouth like small flowers. *The sink will need a good scrub anyway*, she thinks, *before it can be used again*.

With a few minutes to go, Helen cuts a small wedge of strawberry and hands it to Sipsworth in the slipper.

"To perk you up for the next act."

As he turns the fruit in his paws, Helen notices red juice getting all over him.

"I don't suppose they make opera gloves in your size."

Before the curtain rises on act two, Helen nips to the downstairs loo for a bit of toilet paper, which she drops into the slipper.

"If we ever go together for real," she says, "let's bring a hanky, as it's a bit more elegant than fussing with a roll of toilet paper."

Helen imagines them seated in the grand tier; Sipsworth is peering out toward the stage from the back of his slipper, which is black velvet and not tartan. All around them are women in gowns, men in black suits and patent leather shoes. The carpet is thick and feels luxurious to walk on.

"And there's Len . . ." Helen says out loud. "There's my husband."

He's coming back from the toilet, but can't find the row. Helen waves and Len rolls his eyes. He is young, but doesn't look young—because whenever she imagines him, they are the same age.

"You know what he said to me, Sipsworth? That being in the opera house was like being stuck in a bloody great box of chocolates."

When they are back on the couch Helen tries to get Sipsworth into his new house but he won't budge from the slipper. By the closing act of *Rigoletto*, however—as the curtain hangs in readiness—the mouse approaches Helen from the toe of the slipper with a piece of toilet paper in his mouth.

Helen laughs. "The most dramatic climax in all of Italian opera and you're ready for bed? Just like Len. You're like two peas, you and him."

As Gilda's closing aria unspools from radios across the United Kingdom, Helen lowers the slipper into the aquarium. Still holding the paper in his mouth, Sipsworth waddles with tiredness into his pie box and disappears through the hole.

Helen bites her lip. "Wait till the other mice at the shelter hear that you heard *Rigoletto* at the Royal Opera House with Erin Morley as Gilda. That's something to be very proud of."

Going up the stairs, Helen imagines people leaving the performance, moving quietly over wet streets, getting into cabs or hurrying into the bright mouth of the Tube.

In bed, Helen's mind turns to Cecil.

What his life must be like in the shop, day after day after day. The loneliness he keeps private. And that moment the man who he believed was the great love of his life explained how he was going to Spain and would not be returning.

The life they had known together was at an end, except in memory.

Drifting off, Helen sees Cecil in her garden.

It's warm and his shirt is ringed with sweat at the armpits. He's cutting back the bushes and telling Helen about this and that, flowers and bees and wind.

FRIDAY

27.

THE NEXT DAY is bright, with the sharp chill of late autumn blunted by pooling sun in the corners of Helen's home.

After putting on slippers and going through her morning routine in the bathroom, Helen descends the creaky staircase, curious to see how Sipsworth has enjoyed his first night in the new home. She's going to inform Tony in no uncertain terms that Sipsworth is to live in his fish tank at the shelter, as other animals might do him harm on account of his trusting nature.

Waiting for the toast to pop up, Helen is still thinking about Cecil. Specifically the potential for her small garden. Perhaps it wouldn't be a terrible idea to clear things up a bit, cut back the bushes and trees in readiness for spring.

As Helen flicks on the radio (Mozart's *Requiem*), she imagines them out there sunbathing. Sipsworth is visiting, having never ingested the perfume of a young rose. She imagines his cone face poking into the flower. The hall radio takes batteries. She could carry it out on a tray with some refreshments.

Helen is surprised to see Sipsworth awake as she approaches the fish tank with her plate of breakfast toast. Perhaps he is adjusting to her sleep cycle so they can spend time together before he leaves?

But when she looks in, his chest is heaving in and out. His eyes have narrowed—not in the way he squints after waking up, but with an effort that suggests he is struggling to breathe.

"Good god!" Helen exclaims, putting the plate down quickly. She rushes back to the kitchen and cuts a wedge of strawberry, which she brings in and holds up to his face, hoping this heavy breathing is something he can control, and a treat will shake him out of it. But he turns away, his small mouth continuing to open and close like one of the singers from last night's performance.

Helen races into the hall, switches off the radio ("Montagues and the Capulets") and yanks the Yellow Pages from a cupboard. Flicking to the right section, she searches with her finger for an emergency number in one of the boxed ads, then dials.

"County Vet Services, how may I help you?"

"My animal is having some sort of breathing seizure and needs immediate care."

"I'm sorry to hear that," the woman says. "What kind of animal and what is its age?"

"Mouse. Age unknown."

"Oh I'm very sorry, madam, but we don't take exotics."

"For god's sake!" Helen explodes. "How can an animal that inhabits every corner of Britain be *exotic*?"

"I'm deeply sorry, our practice doesn't see anything smaller than a rabbit. But I can give you the numbers for surgeries that see exotics in Oxford and London."

"Let me speak to the vet," Helen says. Her hand is shaking. "Bring the vet to the phone."

"She's not here at the moment, I'm afraid."

"Then why are you taking calls!"

"To book appointments, madam. For later."

"Fine, give me the number of someone, quickly!"

"Where would you . . ."

"Oxford . . . but even that's too far to go with a mouse in his condition."

Helen takes down the number and hangs up without saying goodbye.

When she calls the place on Beaufort Street in Oxford, an answer machine kicks in.

"You are . . ." Helen declares solemnly, "completely and utterly useless."

But once put down, the phone rings. Helen snatches it from the cradle.

"Hello? Hello?"

"Ah, yes, Mrs. Cartwright, this is Tony from Pet Safe . . ."

"OH, BUGGER OFF, TONY!" Helen smashes down the receiver then stares at the phone, daring it to ring again.

She is surprised at herself for losing composure. Even when the police explained what happened to her son as he was crossing the road, she had stood there, nodding. One of the officers brewed a pot of tea. Made her sit down and drink it. Her son's body was at the hospital and at some point she would have to confirm it was him. But she didn't spill a single drop of tea, not a drop.

Helen realises that this might be her first public outburst since the bombs were falling on her town as a child. Oh the fury she felt then, as the sky vibrated with the thrum of approaching enemy aircraft.

But the last thing Sipsworth needs at this moment, Helen reasons, is to hear her upset. Like all children, he might blame himself.

Helen does something then that she hasn't done in years. She stands very still for ten seconds. Breathes. Lets her jaw completely relax. And when the jaw is relaxed, the tongue can go limp. Her hands stop shaking. Her vision sharpens and Helen can feel her mind emerging from the haze of her advanced age, like Excalibur from the lake. It's as though this sudden emergency after three decades of retirement has sharpened her old skills.

She moves calmly to the kitchen, takes a paper and pen from beside the bread bin, and is soon back in the sitting room. Sipsworth is still struggling to breathe, so Helen sits next to him on the couch, counting the number of breaths he takes over sixty seconds, and then multiplying it by his tidal volume for the minute ventilation. She looks around the fish tank for a possible mechanism of injury, such as a piece of glue ingested from the pie box flap. She also scrutinizes his stools for their texture or traces of blood. Helen does this calmly and within two minutes is back in the hall on the telephone.

"Meadowpark Hospital operator. How can I direct your call?"

"Cardiopulmonary, please."

"Yes, right away."

After a few moments of waiting, there is another voice. "Good morning, heart and lung department."

"I need to speak with the attending."

"Dr. Jamal is in a meeting, is it something I can help with?"

"Possibly." Helen says flatly. "I'm at home with a friend who's having an acute respiratory attack and needs help."

"Can you describe what you see?"

"A reliance on accessory muscles, tachypnea, and possible tachycardia."

"Any dizziness or loss of consciousness?"

"L. O. C. unknown," Helen goes on. "Patient is currently alert and oriented, but I'm not sure if the airway is fully patent."

"Give me your name and address. We have our own ambulance service and I'm dispatching medics to your location."

"I've already ordered a taxi," Helen lies. "It'll be quicker." Before the woman can speak, she hangs up the phone and grabs her coat. The phone rings but she ignores it.

It isn't the embarrassment of an ambulance pulling up to the house—lights and sirens blazing—but what might happen when they realise the patient is only five inches tall and covered in fur.

After telephoning for a taxi, Helen stands in the hall considering whether to take Sipsworth or leave him. The danger is that she'll be denied admission by security when they notice what's in her slipper.

When Helen checks on him again, Sipsworth has moved to a corner of the aquarium and is trying to cover himself in bits of toilet paper. A natural instinct, Helen suspects, to protect himself from predators while incapacitated. She closes the curtains, refills his cap of water, and leans into the tank so he can see her clearly. It isn't the first time she has been in a situation like this. And as in theatres of war, while it's easy to be strong in the moment, the silence later will pull you apart.

"I want you to do your best and breathe," she commands. "Don't worry about anything else. Just relax and focus on breathing. I'm going for help."

She takes a small, floral handkerchief from her pocket and puts it into the fish tank. "So you don't forget me." It's a gesture she remembers from a film she saw late one night on BBC One, *The English Patient.*

When the taxi comes, Helen is already at the curb signalling with both hands. A large man behind the wheel is eating.

"Meadowpark Hospital, quick as you can!"

The driver flings his sandwich onto the empty passenger seat and a piece of tomato goes flying. The car lurches violently as he crunches through the gears. The taxi driver is wearing a gold bracelet, and a tattoo on his arm bears the initials E.M. along with a date, written in floral script. When they approach town, the driver flashes his lights at anyone obeying the speed limit, and—after checking for cars—roars through red lights honking his horn. A moment later, as they're overtaking a bread van on the wrong side of the road, the rest of his sandwich flops onto the floor. He ignores it. People out shopping stop and stare.

"Accident and emergency, young lady?"

"No, no, just general admission, if you know where that is."

"Roger that," he says, swerving around a motorized wheelchair in the bike lane. An air freshener hanging from the mirror swings wildly. Helen wonders if it might hit him in the face.

When they stop hard at the entrance, Helen hands the driver a large note and says, "It's people like you who won the war."

28.

HELEN RUSHES TO the desk and asks for the cardiopulmonary wing.

"Visiting hours don't start until . . ."

"I'm a doctor," Helen says. "And it's an emergency."

"Right," says the young woman. "Follow the orange line on the floor, then take the lift to five, they can expedite credentialling up there."

The doors open to a nurses' station and general hospital noise like machines and the rattle of things being wheeled between wards.

Helen is the only person not in a medical uniform. Someone calls to her from the desk. "Can I help you?"

"I hope so," she says, approaching. "I need some supplies to care for a companion who is housebound."

The nurse scrutinizes Helen for a moment, then her eyes soften. "Well, I wish I had a friend like you," she says cheerfully. "I'm Kathy. Why don't you tell me more about what's going on."

Helen inhales slowly. She must stay calm. "I just need a few things and then I'll be on my way."

"Have you tried Boots Chemists on the High Street? They should be open now and have all sorts of items that can help you care for someone in their own home. I can make a list to give the pharmacist if you want."

"No, no," Helen says, waving away the offer. "A pharmacy is no use for what I need."

A nurse nearby stops typing to listen.

"Oh I see," Kathy says, putting a piece of paper and a pen on the counter for the old woman before her. "Why don't *you* make a list then? We always have a few bandages and things floating around, if that would make you feel better."

Helen writes quickly. Two more nurses have gathered and are watching the scene unfold with amusement.

"Here," Helen says, holding up the list when it's finished. "I need all these things. ALL of them." She unclips her purse. Draws out a wad of fifty-pound notes. "I'm happy to pay whatever it costs."

After reading for a few moments, Kathy stands up. Her tone is now serious. "I'm afraid half of these things are controlled substances."

"Yes, yes I know," Helen says, sliding an old, laminated ID card from her purse. "But I'm a doctor."

The nurse takes the card. Looks at the photo of a woman in her late fifties, then at the person standing before her. "Dr. Helen Cartwright," Kathy reads aloud. "Head of Pediatric Cardiology, Sydney General Hospital."

"That's right. Not just an old woman after all."

"Cartwright . . ." Kathy says slowly. "Helen Cartwright . . . why does your name seem familiar?"

"The Cartwright Aortic Stem Valve. I invented it in 1983."

The nurses who had been listening near the desk are now staring. "We had a whole chapter on you in nursing school," one of them says. "But I thought you were . . ."

Helen raises one eye. "Dead? Not quite."

Kathy puts the ID card down and the others look at it. "Dr. Jamal is already on his rounds," she tells Helen, "but I'll go and find him."

"Thank you, nurse. I wish there had been someone like you on my own staff."

Kathy touches a finger to her chin as if remembering something. "You're not the person who called fifteen minutes ago, are you? To say you were coming in a taxi?"

"Yes, that was me."

"The patient isn't with you?"

"No, I left him at home."

"But why?"

"Just please trust me on this, Kathy, it was better he stayed in his . . . bedroom."

The desk nurse nods and goes off.

Helen wonders how Sipsworth is doing at home by himself.

"I wasn't going to say I thought you were dead," the nurse by the desk reassures her. "But that I thought you were Australian."

Helen smiles at the girl. "I suppose I am Australian, in a way."

The sights, sounds, and smells bring back many details of her old life. Helen starts to feel capable again, confident she can administer treatment to save her mouse's life.

× × ×

After a few minutes, Helen sees a man she assumes must be Dr. Jamal. *My god, he's a child,* she thinks. He is striding toward her, studying the list. When they are face-to-face, Helen can see that he is indeed very young for such a senior position. Probably clever and hopefully proud—as this will make him less likely to turn away from a difficult case.

"This is quite a list, Dr. Cartwright," he says. "Wouldn't your friend be more comfortable here with us?"

"I'm not sure he would be suited to a place like this."

"The problem is I can't just give out these things . . . even though you're famous amongst heart surgeons, this is the NHS. You're not licensed in the UK, and it's all paperwork and regulation even for a litre of oxygen."

"I'm happy to return the oxygen tank and regulator, if that's what you're worried about."

Dr. Jamal stares at her for a moment and Helen can tell that he's thinking.

"Why don't we go to the staff cafeteria. They have coffee there and we can talk."

"But I'm in a hurry . . ."

He leans in, and in a low voice says, "I understand that, Dr. Cartwright, but I need to know more if I'm going to *help* you."

Helen follows Dr. Jamal to a bank of lifts. In one room Helen can hear moaning. In another, somebody is watching television. Helen recognizes the voice of the host. The corridor smells like toast and orange juice.

Dr. Jamal pushes the button for the correct floor and the doors close. "I've been using the Cartwright valve since the clinical phase of my training, I can't believe the doctor who invented it is in the lift with me. Now they're talking about 3D-printed valves made from a patient's own cells that grow along with the recipient."

"It's a different world, Dr. Jamal, one in which I'm sure you'll make an impression."

The staff refreshment area is well lit and clean. There are sandwiches and fruit in refrigerated display cabinets. Also, a display of crisps and nutritional bars.

When they reach the register with two hot beverages, Dr. Jamal introduces Helen as one of the most famous cardiologists in the world. The man behind the till taps his chest. "That's very good to know, what with my dodgy ticker."

When they are seated, Dr. Jamal asks about the patient. "Is it your significant other, Dr. Cartwright?"

"No, no," Helen says, trying to find the right words. "But as it might have some bearing on the prognosis, I should probably mention that he's quite small."

Dr. Jamal seems suddenly concerned. "Pediatric?"

"Smaller . . ."

He sits up. "A neonate?" There is panic in his voice now.

"No, no, nothing like that. The patient is naturally small because at this moment in time he happens to be a mouse."

Mohammad Jamal, MD, a decorated physician who trained at University College London, then served as a combat medic before traveling for two years through villages in three developing nations with Médecins Sans Frontières—a physician who sincerely feels he's seen a greater variety of cases than any of his peers from London to Edinburgh—is completely stupefied.

Eventually he manages to speak. "A mouse?"

"That is correct," says Helen. "*Mus musculus.*"

Dr. Jamal looks at his hands. "I see, I see . . . these things on the list are for your friend who is a mouse . . ."

"Exactly. And our patient is obviously suffering from a rodent form of chronic obstructive pulmonary disease, which is causing bronchospasms and hypoxia."

Dr. Jamal takes a deep breath and looks at the list in his hand. "Hence the oxygen tank, albuterol, and ipratropium bromide."

"Any bronchodilator will do, Dr. Jamal. And ipratropium bromide *is* indicated for the treatment of reversible bronchospasm."

Dr. Jamal rubs his eyes. "Jesus, if I *could* get any of this for you, and I'm not saying I can, just hypothetically if I could, Dr. Cartwright, how would you handle dosing, and how were you planning to adjust the non-rebreather?" He shakes his head. "I'm thinking a nasal cannula would be useless."

"Yes, it would," Helen admits, "unless it can be modified."

Dr. Jamal pulls out his phone and scrolls for a few moments. Finally, he turns the screen toward Helen.

"From what you've told me, according to this mouse blog, it sounds like pulmonary mycoplasma," he says, "which I'm guessing is a progressive illness. But we can't be sure without blood work."

"No, Dr. Jamal, that wouldn't do . . . a needle would be the end of him—imagine someone coming at you with a bloody pole vaulter's pole!"

"Well . . ." Dr. Jamal goes on, still looking at his phone. "If it is just a respiratory infection, an antibiotic will clear it up within a few days according to TheDailySqueak.com." He looks at Helen, touches the sleeve of her coat. "This might seem like a stupid question . . ."

"There's no such thing as stupid questions, Dr. Jamal, only stupid answers."

"Well, I was going to ask if you'd considered taking your mouse to a vet?"

"Mice are classified as exotic pets, and the closest surgery is Oxford, and they were closed when I telephoned, with no emergency number on their answer machine."

Dr. Jamal tuts. "No emergency number? That's very unprofessional."

"I knew if I came here, I'd find someone good. Cardiologists have always been the cream of any medical school."

Dr. Jamal clears his throat. "Is the patient at home now?"

Helen nods. "Most likely still gasping for breath."

Dr. Jamal types a number into his phone. "Kathy, it's Mohammad, can you page Dr. McLaverty on D Level and ask her to finish my rounds? It's just routine stuff. I need two hours. Okay. I know. That's today? Jesus. Was it always today? Fine. What time is it happening? Okay. I'll be back by then. One more thing, Kathy: do we still unofficially keep that basket of expired meds under the sharps box in case of a mass casualty incident? Lovely. You're a star, Kathy—I owe you, like, ten Starbucks. Yes, I'm with Dr. Cartwright now."

He hands his phone to Helen, then takes out a pager. "Read this section on mycoplasma pulmonis. Finish your coffee and tell Stanley at the till if you want something else. I'll be back in under ten minutes with some expired medication and a couple of non-rebreathers. How we're going to handle dosing, though, I have no idea. Maybe we can try the vet in Oxford again on the way to your house? There might already be medications for this, and if so, we should defer to them."

Helen nods. "And the oxygen, doctor?"

Dr. Jamal takes a deep breath. "I keep a tank in my car for motor vehicle accidents, which I'm going to let you borrow."

Helen looks at her hands. They are shaking. Dr. Jamal cups them in his. "If we can't take care of our own when the time comes, then what's the point of it all, eh?"

Helen nods, but keeps her eyes fixed on a small ceramic boat with packets of sugar lined up like tiny passengers.

"Oh, and what's the name of the patient, Dr. Cartwright?"

"Sipsworth," she says, feeling the pocket where her handkerchief is usually balled up. "Sipsworth Cartwright."

29.

THE DOCTOR'S CAR is a black Volvo that smells like expensive hand cream. Helen directs him to Westminster Crescent. At a red traffic light, Dr. Jamal calls the number for the exotic vet in Oxford. The sound of ringing through the car's speakers is startling, but Helen knows she'll endure anything to save her mouse.

"Oh, hello there. I wonder if it would be possible to speak to the vet for a few minutes? My name is Dr. Jamal, and I'm head of cardiology at Meadowpark. Yes, of course. I'll hold." He turns to Helen. "How old is Sipsworth?"

"No idea."

"If you had to guess . . ."

"My book says that mice live for about two years, so I would estimate that he's just over one. He has energy—but there's also wisdom."

A woman's voice suddenly fills the car. "Dr. Jamal? This is Vicky Preston, head vet."

"Hello, Dr. Preston. I'm calling on behalf of a . . . colleague who has a sick male mouse, about thirteen months old, presenting with gasping breaths, accessory muscle use. We suspect a respiratory infection or perhaps mycoplasma pulmonis."

"I'm sorry to hear that. Is it a specimen or a pet?"

"The latter . . . a pet."

"Fine, we're the only rodent specialists in the area, and would be happy to help. Why don't you have your colleague bring the animal in for an examination? We won't know if it's mycoplasma unless we run labs. What's his energy level normally?"

Helen gives Dr. Jamal a thumbs up.

"Good, good. Mouse business as usual."

"So whatever we're dealing with is, thankfully, not systemic."

"And hopefully not congenital," adds Dr. Jamal. Helen nods her head in agreement.

"Any excessive scratching?" the vet wants to know.

Helen tilts her hand from side to side.

"Not excessive . . . but there is some, I believe."

"Can your colleague bring him in on Monday morning? When we examine him we'll check for mites, too, as they are often present but don't cause problems unless normal defense mechanisms are weakened."

Helen points to her house and Dr. Jamal parks neatly at the curb.

"Thank you, Dr. Preston. I'll have my colleague call back and make that appointment for Monday."

When they get inside, Helen leads her visitor to the sitting room, where Sipsworth is sleeping outside of his box atop Helen's handkerchief. His eyes are closed and his head is resting at an angle on both paws. Dr. Jamal sets down the medical bag he has brought in.

Helen releases a long breath. "Thank god for that. The attack must have passed."

Dr. Jamal leans in to see the mouse in more detail.

"They're sweet little creatures, aren't they? Is tachypnea normal? I see his body . . ."

"Oh yes," Helen tells him. "Their hearts beat three hundred to seven hundred times a minute."

"To think that such a tiny muscle can work at such a pace for what, two years?"

"Do you believe in God, Dr. Jamal?"

He chuckles. "When I'm in the operating theatre . . ."

"Well, I don't," Helen says abruptly. "Not that it matters one way or another . . . but it's organic engineering like this that keeps me guessing about a higher power."

Dr. Jamal opens his bag of expired medications and equipment. "If it wasn't for mice," he says, "our jobs would be even harder."

Helen turns to the young cardiologist. "There should be a golden mouse statue outside every hospital . . . every time we take a pill or get a vaccination it's all because of mice. Billions must have died over the years in labs, billions! If only people realised," Helen goes on, "that their loved ones are most likely alive or not in pain because of mice."

Dr. Jamal is reading the expiration date on a small tube. "Well, that makes me feel much better about illegally giving you these medicines and oxygen." He then checks the label on a vial of ipratropium bromide. "I forgot to mention that when I read about rodent respiratory diseases on my phone, it said that mycoplasma is not contagious to humans, only other mice. So if that's what your Sipsworth has, he'll have to spend his life alone."

"He has me," Helen mutters. "I'm alone too."

Dr. Jamal takes out his phone. "I'm going to write down the number of the vet in Oxford so you can make an appointment."

"I'll take an express bus from the marketplace. Hopefully they allow mice as passengers." Helen peers down at the small sleeping body. "But maybe there's something the vet could send over today? Just to keep him stable over the weekend . . . perhaps an antibiotic, what harm could it do?"

"There's an idea," Dr. Jamal says. "A bronchodilator wouldn't hurt either if they have one. I'll ring them back."

Helen points. "There's a phone in the hall you can use."

Dr. Jamal paces up and down as he talks to the vet, passing the downstairs loo and the radio many times. When the call ends, he returns to the sitting room.

"Well, it looks like you and Sipsworth are turning us all into criminals. The vet said not to use any medication from the hospital, but to build an oxygen chamber if we can."

"What about mouse drugs?"

"I'm coming to that. The receptionist you called utterly useless on the answer machine will arrive in a few hours on her motorbike with a bag containing a bronchodilator in the form of an oral solution, an oral antibiotic, and several syringes for you to draw and administer the medication to the patient, per os.

"Oh, excellent, excellent," Helen claps. "Now we're really getting somewhere!"

"The receptionist will also bring a bill for the medicine, and something for you to sign to say you were satisfied with the vet's physical examination of your pet, as she's not supposed to give out meds without having been in the same room as the animal. I'm going to take video of Sipsworth now and text it to the vet, so she can at least say in her patient care report that she *saw* him . . . but none of this is strictly kosher."

"Don't you mean halal, Doctor?"

"Yes, very funny," he says. "It's nice to see you smiling for once."

As Dr. Jamal is shooting a video of the sleeping mouse with his phone, he tells Helen that if it is mycoplasma, it's terminal. "The vet said medicine can prolong his life, but eventually, alveolar hypoxia will . . ."

"Yes, I fully understand."

"Of course you do, Dr. Cartwright. Forgive me. I keep forgetting who you are."

They look at the animal lying on Helen's patterned handkerchief. His eyes are closed, but his small, plump body shakes with the speed of his breath. A paw kicks out as if he is in a dream, running from or toward something.

"I'm going to take the expired meds back to the hospital, but leave you some non-rebreathing masks, tubing, a humidifier, and the oxygen tank, which is quite small, so you shouldn't have any trouble maneuvering it."

"Is there a regulator and key?"

"Times have changed, Dr. Cartwright. The regulator is built into the tank, and this one doesn't need a key . . . but bleed it for a second to clear any dust. It's been in the boot with my golf clubs."

Helen promises she'll remember.

"I wish I could stay and help you think of how to build an oxygen chamber, but I'm needed on the ward. Do you have enough money to pay the vet?"

Helen nods. "I have nine hundred thousand pounds in the bank."

"Well, I don't think it's going to be that much . . . but maybe make the woman a sandwich or something? It's a fifty-minute ride from Oxford. And give her a tenner for petrol. Do you have a ten-pound note?"

"Yes, of course, in my handbag. But I should give *you* something . . ."

Dr. Jamal closes his bag with all the expired medicines inside. "Now that's definitely my cue to leave."

Helen sees him to the door and when they are on the step, she says, "You're a good doctor, Dr. Jamal, not because you're so clever—but because your first instinct is still to help."

"Well, thanks to you, I can now add 'Outlaw' to my CV. Please don't tell anybody about that oxygen tank. There are administrators at Meadowpark who would love to see me put a foot wrong."

As she watches Dr. Jamal zoom off in his big car, Helen imagines him as an elderly man with a cane, appearing on the floor of her old cardiology wing at Sydney General—and then the duty nurse calling Helen over in the middle of her morning rounds.

Would she have listened to his story?

There were times, Helen realises then, that she could probably have been kinder to people.

30.

FOR THE NEXT two hours, Helen sits on the couch observing her mouse with the television and radio off. Then she has an idea. Gets up and goes into the hall. In a drawer is the receipt for the glue traps she bought last Saturday. Helen dials a number written at the bottom and listens to it ring.

"Hardware. Cecil speaking."

"It's Helen Cartwright."

"Oh, Mrs. Cartwright, how's the mouse?"

"Terrible, which is why I'm calling."

An hour later, a white van pulls up outside Helen's house on Westminster Crescent. Cecil is carrying a clear plastic tub packed with things. He has also brought a case with a drill and some other tools.

Helen swings open the door before he can knock. "Hello there missus and how is his lordship?"

"Still sleeping on my handkerchief, so please bring all that into the hall so as not to wake him."

"What about the carpet?"

"Oh, bugger the carpet! It'll outlive us all."

Cecil takes off his coat, then just stands there looking at the things he's brought.

"Sorry I can't offer you tea," Helen says. "But the noise . . . it might start another attack."

"I had a cup before I arrived. Now, where were you thinking you'd want this thing?"

"In the sitting room. But can we build it in the hall? I'll go and get the oxygen equipment from the other room."

When she returns, Cecil has opened the lid of the plastic tub. There are all sorts of new mouse toys and a big bag of fluff for bedding.

"What's all this, Cecil?"

"Years ago when I was in hospital, Ian brought a few things to cheer me up. I thought I'd do the same for Mr. Sipsworth."

"That was very thoughtful of you."

"Not at all. May I see the oxygen tubing please, Mrs. Cartwright?"

Helen watches him inspect a length of the sterile plastic and select a drill bit. Then he holds something up from the pile of things Helen has dropped near his tools.

"What on earth is this?"

"It attaches to the non-rebreathing mask to humidify the oxygen."

"Ah," Cecil says, hesitating. "So running a line from the tank to the tub is not going to work."

"We don't *have* to humidify the oxygen," Helen says. "It just might be more comfortable for him."

"Do you need access to the humidifier once the oxygen is running?"

"No, not until it runs out."

"So, I can use this mask thingy, but place it inside the tub? I'm just concerned about getting a good seal."

"Do whatever you think is best," Helen says. "And whatever it costs, I don't care."

Cecil wraps a rag around the body of the drill to muffle the noise. Soon there is a small hole in the lid of the plastic tub. Cecil points to the sticker of a baby next to the word DANGER.

"These tubs are airtight, so you can't put the lid on unless the oxygen tank is running . . . do you want me to write that down?"

"No, thank you."

Cecil gets up and fumbles in his shop-coat pockets for a pen and paper. "Well, all the same," he says. "It's more for me than you." Helen watches him write on a piece of paper the sentence DO NOT CLOSE LID UNTIL OXYGEN IS FOWLING.

He uses clear tape to attach the note to the top of the box. "Just so I can sleep at night," he says. "Oh Lord! I've spelled *flowing* wrong!"

"For god's sake," Helen says. "It's fine."

Cecil slips a cardboard picture of a small rabbit from the pile of things in the tub. "I cut this from a box of toilet paper. I did some research and found that mice get along with rabbits, especially mini lops. Thought it might be nice for Sipsworth to have a friend in there.

Helen stares at the shopkeeper. "You're a very empathetic person, Cecil."

He laughs. "Is that why I'm alone?"

"Don't talk nonsense. Your customers idolize you, you're treasurer at the bowls club, plus you have an old woman and a mouse whose life is now in your hands."

Cecil tapes the cardboard rabbit to the inside of the tub. After that, he fills it with fluff and sets in a few of the new toys he has brought.

Helen excuses herself to check on Sipsworth. The mouse is still laid out on the handkerchief, exhausted. She creeps over to check he is breathing and remembers her book: "Mice always sleep where they feel most comfortable—usually in boxes or hiding places." To be out in the open like this, Helen realises, means he must have complete faith in her. She presses her lips together, determined not to let him down.

When she gets back to the hall, Cecil is scratching his large head.

"This is the tricky bit," he tells her. "Attaching the mask and humidifier so that you can get them out for cleaning. Tape won't work because the humidity levels will cause it to loosen . . . and then the whole thing could come crashing down."

"What are you going to do then?"

Cecil pulls out a tool that resembles a hypodermic needle and she watches him begin to feed bits of plastic-coated wire through tiny holes in the lid. "I'm going to suspend it."

There is a knock at the door. Helen retrieves her handbag from the hall table. "With any luck, that'll be the vet's assistant."

Standing outside is a woman in her twenties wearing all leather. A red motorcycle is parked at the curb behind Cecil's white van.

"Are you the woman with the mouse?" she asks.

"Yes, Dr. Helen Cartwright. Please come in, though I ask that you speak softly. It's been a hard morning and he's finally asleep."

The young woman has a white bag in one hand and her phone in the other.

Helen leads her into the kitchen, past Cecil, who is still threading wire through the lid.

"Ooh, looks like you're making the oxygen chamber. I'll tell Dr. Preston." She holds up the bag. "Medicine and oral syringes."

In the kitchen, they open the bag and lay its contents between the toaster and the sink.

"So, you'll want to shake this before you give it to him. Pull it up into the oral syringe to the correct dose, 0.05 mL for both. If you have an air bubble, start again. Same goes for the antibiotic."

Helen nods. "Does it need to be refrigerated?"

"No, but don't leave it in direct sunlight." The vet's assistant takes out a piece of paper from her jacket pocket. "Here's the invoice. If you could sign and date. I'll also need to take another video of Sipsworth."

Helen takes her through to the sitting room, where Sipsworth is drinking from the bottle cap.

"He's up!" Helen cries. "He's up!"

Sipsworth raises his head to the sound of Helen's voice and blinks one eye.

"He's lovely," the woman says, holding out her camera. "What a gorgeous creature."

"And a very good boy," Helen adds, peering in. "Aren't you, Sips?"

"Hopefully it was just an isolated episode, though Dr. Preston said that with an infection he could have intermittent attacks for a few days. So best to finish the course of meds—but you'll be coming in before then, I think?"

"First thing Monday. Do you have a card with the surgery address? I'll be coming from the bus station."

"No, you will not!" Cecil is standing in the doorway, arms akimbo. He turns to the vet's assistant. "I'll bring them in the van."

After Helen hands over a cheque for the surgery and some money for food and petrol, the young woman darts off on her motorbike.

Cecil has finished and is packing away the tools. "As my mother always said, it takes a village. And it's good people see vehicles parked outside your house, what with all the break-ins happening at the moment. You might want to think about having a security system installed once we've got Sipsworth sorted. Can't be too careful nowadays."

Helen nods. "But I really have nothing of value, Cecil . . ."

"There's the television for one . . . plus I'm sure you've got family heirlooms. Burglars love those. Do you want me to take some measurements? See where we could pop a camera?"

"That's very kind of you, but I'd rather we focus on getting Sipsworth back to full strength."

"I have a feeling he'll be right as rain by next week, missus. Nature's funny like that, righting its own wrongs. Now, let me show you how Britain's first mouse oxygen chamber works . . ."

It is decided that Cecil's lifesaving contraption should sit on a thick cushion next to the French door.

"Turn on the oxygen first . . ." Helen reminds herself, "so it's going before the lid is on."

"*Co*rrect," Cecil says, noticing the misspelling on his sign. "You must think me a right idiot, you being a doctor an' all."

"Anyone who can build a custom oxygen chamber in less than an hour is by no means an idiot, though you might be dyslexic, Cecil."

× × ×

After he's gone, Helen makes something to eat, then creeps to the couch because Sipsworth is sleeping again. The sitting room is quite dark. When she turns on the television, his small body seems to glow.

There's a good film on ITV, a comedy. A man's late wife has come back from the dead to live with him and his new bride after a séance goes wrong.

Every now and then, Helen glances down to check on Sipsworth. Her plan is to administer all meds the moment he stirs.

By the time *Newsnight* is over on BBC Two, the mouse is still snoozing. Helen doesn't think she can stay up much longer, and lays her head on a cushion with the idea of closing her eyes just for five minutes.

SATURDAY

31.

THE NEXT MORNING Helen wakes up on the couch. She's fully dressed and the television is on. Sipsworth is in the midst of another gasping attack, with his chest going like mad, and his glassy eyes bulging with each inhalation. His small face looks ragged, as if he's been in a fight, which makes Helen suspect the attack started in the early hours. It is taking every ounce of energy for him to breathe—which means there'll be no way to get medicine into his body until the attack has ceased.

If the mouse has mycoplasma of the lungs, his heart will eventually give out from the sustained effort—or he'll drown as his lungs slowly fill with fluid from within. Helen remembers the vet's assistant telling her how even a mild infection could cause these breathing episodes to last awhile.

Then she remembers Cecil's oxygen chamber. It's on a cushion by the French door. Helen reaches into the aquarium and boldly scoops the mouse in one motion.

Sipsworth doesn't fight or try to scramble away once he's lowered into the plastic tub.

"In a few moments, you're to going to feel a draft, Sipsworth. Don't be alarmed—it's just oxygen, pure oxygen."

After filling the humidifier with room-temperature water from the kettle, Helen turns the green dial and adjusts the flow to twelve litres of oxygen a minute, then snaps on the lid.

As oxygen flows, she watches her mouse through the clear plastic, but after a minute the walls of the tub begin to swell. Cecil has made a mistake. Helen unlatches the lid. Twists the oxygen off. Rushes to the kitchen for a sharp knife. Takes Sipsworth from the tank and puts him into one of her slippers. She can't find his anywhere and there's no time to look.

With her mouse safely out of the way, Helen punctures the side of the tub—stabbing from the inside out to minimize the risk of sharp edges that might cut him.

A moment later, Sipsworth is back in the chamber with the oxygen flowing. When the sides begin to swell, Helen turns the flow down to eight litres per minute as air whistles through the holes.

After twelve minutes, the gasping attack stops.

Sipsworth, weak and disheveled, makes his way across the fluff to the side of the tub and puts his nose into one of the holes. It is pink and very small.

"Good boy!" Helen cries, carefully removing the lid, then turning the regulator down to zero.

She lowers her hand and Sipsworth crawls right in. Helen raises him to eye level, then kisses the top of his body where the fur is coarse and matted. She places him into one of her slippers, then rushes into the kitchen for the bag of medicines and a peanut.

Carefully, Helen pulls up 0.05 mL of the bronchodilator solution into the syringe. "Don't go to sleep just yet, please . . . stay awake if you can."

But the moment she lowers the syringe, he bolts into the toe of her slipper.

"Bugger." Helen moves the syringe even closer, but Sipsworth is pushing himself against the tartan fabric to get away. She puts down the syringe and holds out the peanut to calm him down. Tiny paws reach from the darkness, but Helen retracts the nut because she has an idea. Once the syrupy contents of the first syringe have been squeezed onto her finger, Helen lowers her hand into the slipper where Sipsworth is hiding. He creeps forward, sniffs, then proceeds to lick the medicine vigorously off her skin—even reaching with both paws to hold Helen's finger in place. When it's all gone, she breaks off a fragment of peanut as a reward. Helen does exactly the same thing with the antibiotic. Sipsworth slurps it up, then sniffs around in readiness for his treat.

"You need to sleep now my dear . . . but if you're not up by the late afternoon, I'll have to rouse you for another dose of the medicines."

When she puts him back into the fish tank, Sipsworth scoots over to the lemonade cap for a long drink.

"Don't worry about your appearance . . . you should have seen me when I was hoisted out of that disused well. Sleep now and have a good groom later. I'll put a film on, and we can share a whole strawberry for supper if you like."

When Sipsworth is curled up on her handkerchief, Helen creeps into the kitchen and fills the kettle, desperate for a cup of tea. She's hungry, too, and while two pieces of bread brown in the toaster, Helen stares at the rubbish on her patio.

"If only we can get through winter," she says quietly. "I could clear the garden with the help of Cecil, then we'd be free to spend the warmest days out there in our slippers, like two holidaymakers . . . yes . . . chilled peanut crumbles and cucumber for Sips, lemonade and biscuits for me. And Dr. Jamal could come over . . ." Helen imagines him holding a glass of lemonade, telling her about an upcoming surgery. Maybe they could talk through cases that trouble him. Cecil would like him. They'd be fast friends. Helen imagines herself watching their bowls game from the tea room, trying not to show any favouritism.

After scraping a thin film of margarine across her toast, Helen takes her plate to the French door, still dreaming about all that's possible. There might be other mouse enthusiasts in the town. Surely she isn't the only one. She could share the oxygen chamber with any rodents in need. Maybe there's even a young musophile who hopes of going into medicine. With her mind still intact, Helen could help with homework. She turns to the sunken cushions on her couch. Imagines herself next to a teenager, papers all over the table, talking through fractions and the placement of decimal points as mice frolic in a slipper.

In the afternoon, Helen brings out the Yellow Pages. Flicks to the right section, then dials the number, hoping the sound of her voice won't wake Sipsworth from his medically induced slumber.

"Hello there," says a voice. "How may I help you?"

"I was in the other day for a book on mice, and now I find myself in need of more books, which I believe may have to be ordered."

"Oh, Mrs. Cartwright!"

"You remember me?"

"Of course. Dominic has been asking after you. Do you remember Dominic?"

"Yes, of course I remember him."

"Well, he's got it into his head that you are going to bring your mouse to our coffee hour."

"He's a bit under the weather at the moment. It's the reason I'm calling."

"Oh, what a shame. I'm sure we'd all love to meet him. Is he on the mend?"

"I hope so. Now may I give you the titles of the books I need? I've taken them from the bibliography of the book I currently have on loan."

"Yes, Mrs. Cartwright, fire when ready."

"The first is *The Biology and Medicine of Rabbits and Rodents*, second edition."

Helen listens to her type it in, one key at a time.

"We can get that one in two days, Mrs. Cartwright."

"Fine, thank you. The second book is *Molecular Biology and Pathogenicity of Mycoplasmas*."

"Oh, you might need to help me with the spelling on that one."

Once it's fingered in, the librarian tells Helen that an interlibrary loan edition is currently at the Bodleian in Oxford, so it could take a week. "And you might need a doctor to help you understand this one, Mrs. Cartwright."

"I am a doctor. A cardiac surgeon, to be exact."

There's a pause, then the librarian says quietly, "Oh my goodness . . . wait until I tell Dominic. He's always playing with the anatomical models in our medical learning alcove. Maybe you could sit with him one day and explain what each thing does?"

Helen doesn't speak, but then remembers that Dominic is her son; he belongs to his mother the way David belonged to her.

"What days is Dominic there?"

"Only three days officially, but he usually comes in on his days off. We just don't ask him to do anything."

"Perhaps when I pick up my books, then?"

"Oh, Dr. Cartwright, that's so generous. I should mention that we can also get your books digitally, so you can read them on a tablet or computer. Would that interest you?"

"Certainly not!"

A moment after Helen says goodbye to the librarian, the phone rings. Helen looks at the receiver then lifts the handle cautiously.

"Hello?"

"It's Cecil, Mrs. Cartwright. I was just calling to check in on his lordship."

"I'm sorry to say that when I woke up he was having a very bad attack."

"Oh, dearie me."

"But when I put him in your oxygen chamber, he was soon breathing normally and I was able to give him the medicine."

"Now that's what I call good news."

"For the record, Cecil. At a few minutes before ten o'clock this morning, you saved a young mouse's life."

"Not me, missus, that'll be the pure oxygen what did that. But in more good news, I've been reading up on the catch-and-release systems, and will be demonstrating them to customers on the counter using a marshmallow."

"You'll have to come over, Cecil, so Sipsworth can thank you personally."

"Just give me a ring when he's got enough strength for visitors. And have a think about getting a proper security system. There was another break-in last night on the French estates."

× × ×

Helen wonders if she should call Dr. Jamal. Thank him for yesterday and offer an update. But he's probably already with patients, and Helen is wary of leaving any message that might suggest she has an illegal oxygen tank.

"He'll call later, I'm sure," she tells herself. "Or perhaps I'll visit him at hospital."

She imagines handing over a box of chocolates, or going into Banbury and buying him a Rolex watch like the one Len always wanted. Why not? Why hold anything back? The time in her life for restraint has now passed.

Sipsworth is fast asleep when Helen goes to check on him. She wants to put the telly on, but instead takes off her slippers and lies down on the couch with her head on a cushion and her mouse just a few inches away.

She closes her eyes and goes over her conversation with the librarian, imagining herself there on a chair sitting quietly with Dominic.

The thought melts into a dream, and Helen imagines herself back in theatre with her old team at Sydney General. But when she looks down, instead of seeing the sternum freshly sawn open and the ribs spread with a thoracic retractor, it's the body of a mouse. Helen turns to the tray of sterilized tools and then to her team. The mouse has been sedated and awaits the first incision.

Helen is then in the waiting room. There is no sound. It's 1980-something, and she is explaining to a mother and father how their three-year-old boy in post-op will soon wake up and go home to his bedroom with the many colourful things that are familiar and precious to him. The panic is over. With a new valve, he'll live a normal life.

Now Helen is hovering over a city. It could be Sydney, but she's not sure. It's neither cold nor windy, just very still, and down below there are people in offices, on trains, sipping coffee, talking into mobile phones, falling in love, falling out of love, trying on shoes in shops—alive because of an old woman, far away in England, who has recently adopted a mouse, turned vegetarian, broken the law, and gotten a library card . . . as though preparing to start her life all over again.

32.

WHEN HELEN WAKES from her nap, Sipsworth is still sleeping. She decides to put on the telly at a low volume. Children's programmes will be playing, and Helen wonders if the sound of cartoons and laughter might be comforting, as animals are really just children that never grow up.

Helen gets up quietly with the intention of making tea. Turns off the radio in the hall. Boils the kettle. Takes down a half-empty packet of digestive biscuits from the kitchen cupboard. When she returns to the sitting room, Sipsworth is up and drinking from the lemonade cap. He hears Helen and turns, squinty-eyed but breathing normally, thank god. Helen puts her plate and mug on the carpet, then rushes back to the kitchen. The medicine is first pulled into the syringe, then pushed out onto separate fingers. She hurries back to see Sipsworth drinking again. Once he's finished, Helen offers the bronchodilator first. Gripping her finger with both paws the way a baby holds its bottle, the mouse licks every drop.

Helen whistles joyfully. "Definitely a doctor's child."

With both doses safely ingested, Sipsworth scampers onto the blue castle and waves his front paws. Helen lowers her hand and the mouse pops in with a little leap.

"Take it easy now," Helen warns. "No acrobatics, and certainly no foot racing on that wheel."

Helen spots his missing slipper on the arm of the couch. At first the mouse is reluctant to leave the warmth of her palm, but then he sniffs at something familiar in the heel and stretches his body toward it. Once he's certain it is in fact a peanut, his back legs leave the safety of Helen's hand and he's in the slipper.

"You eat that while I have my tea," she tells him, breaking a digestive biscuit in two.

When the children's programmes have finished, an Australian soap opera comes on. Sipsworth appears from the toe and stands on his back legs.

Helen nods at the screen. The characters in the programme are arguing about how to organize a wedding reception. "Funny you should be interested in this, because it's happening in Australia. Where I used to live with David and Len."

Sipsworth sniffs the air in a way that makes his head nod.

"That's exactly how people talk in Australia. And those birds chattering in the trees, we used to hear them from the terrace. And all that sunlight . . ." Helen goes on. "The streets down there are washed clean with it every day."

She looks at her small friend. He's on his bottom now, licking the fur on his belly.

"I like that we have radio in the morning and telly in the afternoon. A whole day of either is a bit draining."

When a character laughs, Helen turns to the flickering image—the made-up lives that for so long have kept her going.

"Reminds me of my wedding to Len. Of course, we didn't appreciate it on the day. Too busy looking after everyone else, you know, saying hello and all that . . . I hardly saw him after we exchanged vows. And on our wedding night we collapsed into bed and fell asleep in our clothes. Not even a peck on the cheek."

Helen takes a crumb of biscuit. Holds it out.

"Go on . . . a bit of sugar is good for the brain," she says, watching him munch eagerly. "But when you're better, we'd best stick with fruit, because it has fibre in it, along with many other things essential for longevity."

When the show ends, Sipsworth is sitting very still like a small loaf. Helen wonders if the position is somehow comfortable for him, given his respiratory condition.

"There's a jolly good film on Channel 4 tonight. Be nice if we could watch it together—though if you want to sleep, I understand. The medicine is going to make you feel drowsy."

Helen considers putting him back in the oxygen chamber for a spell. Perhaps later, before bed. Give him a head start on the night.

Halfway through the six o'clock news, Helen blinks her eyes. Realises she was dozing and that it's dinnertime.

Sipsworth is curled into a fluffy crescent shape, asleep in the heel of the slipper. Both eyes are closed, which Helen's mouse book says is a sign of trust.

In the kitchen, she opens the cupboard but isn't sure what she wants. So many things look appealing. Why not put out a bit of a spread? It could be like Christmas back home, when the table would be crammed with things both savoury and sweet—the three of them just helping themselves when they felt like it. One

Christmas in particular Helen remembers Len and David on the patio building a quite complicated remote-controlled car from a kit. She was in the lounge, blinds drawn against the blazing sunshine, watching . . . *The Wizard of Oz.* Yes, that was it. And when Helen began to sing, instead of coming in to laugh at her, husband and son hovered in the doorway. David was spinning a miniature wheel and his father was holding the screwdriver.

Don't stop, luv, Len said, when she noticed them watching. *It's lovely.*

That would be their last Christmas, just the three of them.

The intensity of this memory—so close that Helen might take a single step and be there with them—makes her determined to put on a nice spread. Why not? Sipsworth needs fattening up and she could do with a few more calories herself to get through winter.

Helen turns on the oven and opens the freezer for crispy cheese pancakes, vegetable samosas, and little Greek pies with feta and spinach. She removes the packaging and puts everything on the same tray.

There's a giant bag of crisps in the top cupboard and Helen pours some into a bowl. Then she makes several rounds of toast, covering each in a thick tongue of margarine. When that's ready she makes a spread for her mouse, which includes oats, a broken biscuit, lettuce, two blueberries, a quarter strawberry, half an unsalted cashew, and one whole crushed peanut. Helen puts each thing into a different saucer then sets it onto the tray, which she carries into the sitting room.

Sipsworth is still dozing, so Helen clears the coffee table and lays out the little plates of things. With the aroma of food unfurling through the house, the mouse turns over, yawns, then opens both eyes.

33.

With everything laid out, she finally sits down. There is only a minute or so before the film starts on Channel 4, but Helen doesn't want to start filling a plate until she's invested in the story.

Sipsworth is up and biting the fur on his left leg.

"This has turned into a party. Back in Australia we'd have to pull down all the blinds because of the heat, and it would feel like we were in the cinema. My husband had a great knowledge of all the film stars, you know. Say the name of any picture, and he'd rattle off the people in it and if they were any good."

When the movie begins, Helen sits back and pulls her legs up under a cushion.

Names appear one by one on a black screen.

Sipsworth disappears into the toe.

"Where are you going? What about your supper?"

The film is about an American woman with red hair in her fifties who goes to Venice because she's lonely and hopes to find the love that has always eluded her. Helen has seen it before. The actress is Katharine Hepburn. At the beginning she's awkward, and the Italian way of doing things unnerves her.

Helen takes an empty plate and fills it with crisps, one crispy pancake, a samosa, plus a few limp lettuce leaves just to be healthy.

After fifteen minutes, Sipsworth appears. Leans over the side of the slipper toward the food.

"I knew your stomach would bring you out eventually." When Helen reaches down to stroke his fur, Sipsworth clings onto her fingers. She turns her hand and he hops into the open palm.

"Just this once you can roam the table and have whatever you please."

But when she puts the mouse down between the plates, he freezes.

"What's wrong?"

Helen lowers her hand and he scampers back in.

"Fine," Helen says, putting him into the slipper. "You wait there and I'll just bring you little bits and pieces, like tapas."

The first morsel is a piece of nut, which the mouse takes politely and eats, looking at her.

"We should do something like this for Christmas. We could even invite some people this year, Sipsworth."

Helen counts them on her fingers. "There's Cecil, Dr. Jamal, and the librarian could bring Dominic. For some reason, I think you two will get along. We can ask him about our solar system . . . and if there are any planets other than Earth that are suitable for mice."

It occurs to Helen then that Sipsworth might not live to see Christmas, yet the current strength of his appetite assuages concern.

When Katharine Hepburn's character falls into a canal, people rush to help.

Helen picks up a small Greek pie and laughs. "It's because she's in love with the man who works in the gift shop. She's trying to get his attention."

The last scene is of the heroine on a train. A woman who knows she is moving away from the best part of her life toward the version in memory that'll come to define her. She watches Venice in the distance, growing smaller and smaller, then turns away before it can disappear to nothing.

By the time she wakes up, it's close to eleven and all the serious news programmes are coming to an end. When Helen realises she's been sleeping again, she panics and looks for the slipper. Sipsworth has sausaged his body lengthwise, head on his paws. His eyes are open, but he doesn't seem to be looking at anything in particular.

Helen decides not to put him in the oxygen chamber, as he seems relaxed, and the abrupt transition might sour his mood. When her father came back from the war, he would sometimes sleep the whole day. Helen would take his meals in on a tray, and he would just sit there in bed looking at her, not smiling or frowning—just staring at his daughter. If he wanted to hold her hand, she didn't mind.

Helen is too tired to clear away all the food. It can stay on the table all night, she decides, like in Miss Havisham's house.

When she sits up, the cushion moves and the mouse turns his head. He has an elegant, almost aristocratic face when the fur is groomed. Helen puts out two fingers and strokes the side of his body. His eyes partially close on contact, and she can hear his teeth crunching, which Helen's library book says is an indication of bliss.

"Bugger it," she whispers. "You might not live to see Christmas, so there's no reason why you can't sleep upstairs in your slipper next to me."

Then, she thinks, *if there's another attack, he'll have the comfort of seeing a familiar face.*

Helen stands. Takes the slipper in both hands. The mouse yawns and stretches out one paw.

"You know what your gift to the world is, Sipsworth?" Helen asks him. "It's that you bring out the best in people."

There's a dull ache in her back and the stairs feel longer than usual. She has to grip the banister, but Helen balances the slipper in her other hand without any shaking.

"Tomorrow morning after your medicine, we'll take a bath. You can sit beside me on a chair. The heat will soothe my old frame and the steam may be good for your air passages. Not too warm, mind you . . . hot weather is very dangerous to mice. So if we take a holiday when you're fully recovered, we might go to the west country . . . but you'll never see Venice like Katharine Hepburn. Devon's lovely and not that far. I don't suppose you've ever been to the seaside. We might even convince Cecil to come, if he's not too busy with his bowls."

From the corner of her bedroom, Helen lifts a chair she has never sat in and places it next to her bed. Sets the slipper down. Sipsworth is dead asleep, but whatever takes place in the coming darkness, he will not go through it alone.

Helen shoulders into her nightgown and slips between the cool sheets. "I'm going to sleep next to you tonight," she says to the slipper. "We'll be like two mice in a mouse hole."

Helen shuffles her head until she's comfortable on the pillow. Reaches for the bedside lamp and flicks it off.

"Above all . . . don't worry. From now on, any storm we'll weather as a family. In sickness and in health, Len and I said . . . and now I'm saying it to you."

Helen leans in so her face is only inches from the lump in the slipper.

"And if it comes time for the long journey, Sipsworth, don't be afraid. Any mice you knew before, you will see again when they were at their best. Resist any fear," she goes on, her own eyes closing. "I won't be there when you arrive . . . but if you happen to see someone who looks like me, that'll be David. He knows who you are and will be waiting for you. Len will be there, too, with a slipper and fresh peanuts. They'll take you in and look after you. I want you to let them know that I'm fine. I wasn't for a long time, but I am now."

SUNDAY

34.

Cecil has been knocking for almost ten minutes when another car pulls up and parks behind his white van. The man who gets out is wearing khaki trousers and holding a box of chocolates. He waves at Cecil in greeting, then joins him at Helen's front door.

"Is she not home?"

Cecil shakes his head. "Though she may be in the back garden. It's an unseasonably warm day."

The other man raises a hand toward Cecil. "What a storm last week though, eh? I'm Mohammad Jamal."

"Cecil Parks. Pleased to meet you, sir. I take it you know Dr. Cartwright?"

"She came to the hospital where I work, wanting some help for her . . . friend."

Cecil clears his throat. "You mean Sipsworth?"

Dr. Jamal laughs. "So, you know about all this mouse business?"

"I built his lordship's oxygen chamber."

"That's marvelous. Did the vet send over medications?"

"By motorcycle courier, no less. A girl in all leather." Cecil motions toward his van. "I'm taking them to the surgery in Oxford tomorrow but just thought I'd pop over for half an hour, install one of those motion-activated security lights in the back garden."

Dr. Jamal nods his approval. "How long have you been knocking?"

Cecil raises both eyebrows to indicate a length of time, and the two men stand looking at the mustard door.

"I should probably see about getting her a bell," Cecil adds, stepping forward to knock again. Dr. Jamal bends down and peers through the letterbox.

"It's very dark. Doesn't look like the curtains have been pulled."

Cecil glances at his wristwatch. "Oh dear. And past noon. She must be having a lie-in."

The two men face each other, neither willing to say out loud what's on their minds. Then Cecil has an idea.

"How about we try and get round the back? Have a look inside? Make sure she doesn't need any help. Though . . . if she's just popped out for a newspaper and a loaf of bread, we're going to look mighty foolish."

Dr. Jamal sets the box of chocolates on Helen's doorstep. "It's the curtains that worry me."

There is a tall gate at the side of Helen's house, but it's sealed tight against the fence, with all three hinges visibly decayed. Generations of cobwebs bulge from seams of horizontal plank.

Cecil fingers the rough skin of flaking metal. "Oh Lordy, I don't think it's been opened in decades."

The gate is locked from the inside, and too high for either man to reach around.

Dr. Jamal takes off his jacket. "I think our only option is to climb over."

Cecil grunts. "By *our* I'm hoping you mean *you*, as my climbing days are long gone."

Dr. Jamal shows Cecil how to stand with his back to the gate, fingers interlaced to form a step. "At least that's how we did it in the army. I take a run up, lift my foot into your hands, then you lob me over. On three?"

"Oh bugger!" Cecil says. "Be careful."

Dr. Jamal goes back a few paces then gallops at Cecil, trapping his shoe in the shopkeeper's hands, as he's launched skyward to the sound of ripping fabric.

"Bollocks, I'm stuck!"

Cecil shuffles beneath with his arms out. "What can I do?"

"I'm caught on a nail but if I move, I'll fall."

"Are you injured?"

"Apart from my trousers, no. It's much higher than it looks!"

"Oh!" Cecil exclaims. "I have a ladder in the van!"

Dr. Jamal bites his tongue. "Well, can you get it?"

As Cecil is fetching the ladder, a small red car pulls up. It parks slowly in front of his white van. A well-dressed elderly lady gets out, followed by a small round man holding some books.

Cecil meets them on the path to Helen's front door.

"We're from the local library," the woman says. "We've brought Dr. Cartwright a book she ordered, plus a few that Dominic believes she might enjoy on marsupials."

"I don't think she's home," Cecil explains.

"Oh, what a shame . . . Dominic was hoping to meet her mouse."

"He's a charmer, all right." Cecil points to the figure teetering atop the side fence. "Will you excuse me for a moment? I have to rescue someone."

As Cecil hurries off, the ladder banging against his large frame, the librarian and her son continue to the front door, knocking three times, oblivious to what they were just told and to everything going on at the side of the house.

As they wait, Dominic picks up the heart-shaped box of chocolates and lays them atop the three books he has brought.

A moment later the door opens slowly to reveal a dazed, hunched figure in robe and slippers.

"Yes, what is it?" Helen says, squinting into the bright noon light.

The librarian stands to one side and points at her son. "Dominic has a special delivery, if it's not an inconvenient time."

"Books?" Helen says, trying to understand what's happening. "Chocolates?"

"Oh, and Dominic was hoping to meet your mouse."

"He's still fast asleep," Helen mumbles, "but come inside."

She hurries upstairs for the slipper. It's on her chair exactly where she remembers putting it. Sipsworth is deep in the toe, curled into a soft crescent.

Helen's left arm is numb as though still in slumber, so she collects the slipper with her other hand and takes it downstairs to where the librarian and her son are waiting in the doorway. She feels winded from all this sudden action, but manages a few words: "You'll have to excuse us . . . we're not used to visitors so early."

"Oh goodness," says the librarian, "I'll think you'll find it's fast approaching one o'clock."

Helen tuts. "Would you mind closing the front door?"

"Yes, of course, though I do believe someone is being rescued from the side of your house."

The pain in Helen's back returns. A deep thudding ache. If it wasn't for all these people in her hall, she'd go upstairs and sink into a hot bath.

Helen pokes her head out the front door to see Dr. Jamal followed by Cecil, who is carrying a ladder. Both men are breathless.

"There she is!" booms Cecil, setting down the ladder. "We were worried sick."

"About me?" Helen says, looking into the slipper to see if all this fuss has wakened her mouse.

A strip of torn fabric hangs down Dr. Jamal's leg, revealing a hairy thigh.

"What on earth is going on?" Helen demands. "One minute I'm asleep, the next thing I know there's a riot in the front garden!"

"I just came over to see how you were doing," says Dr. Jamal, looking at the others. "I think we all did."

But Helen is still confused. She points to the ladder. "Then what's with the Tower of Babel?"

Cecil shoves both hands into his pockets and shuffles his feet. "Truth be told, I had a dream you were burgled and someone took Sipsworth . . . which I believe was nature's way of telling me to install a motion-activated security light in your back garden."

Helen is about to say something when the librarian holds up her right wrist. "It *is* almost one in the afternoon."

Just then, Sipsworth appears. He is up on both back legs sniffing the outside air. There is no indication whatsoever of any respiratory distress.

Dominic's face opens at the sight of the small animal.

"Well then," Helen sighs. "I suppose you'd better all come in."

She guides the herd through the hall and into the sitting room, holding her slipper aloft with Sipsworth in the heel like some tiny circus animal leading a parade.

"Why don't you all sit down," Helen instructs her guests, still incredulous that everyone has converged en masse. All the food from her impromptu party is still out, and Dominic is piling crisps into his hand.

Cecil whistles. "Looks like you were expecting us, missus! Those are . . . mini samosas, if I'm not mistaken?"

Helen gestures at the many plates of things. "Help yourselves . . . though I warn you, it's been out for a while."

Cecil pats his stomach. "Don't worry about that. Cast iron, this is!"

After lowering Sipsworth into his tank, Helen excuses herself to change out of her nightgown.

Going up the stairs she can hear everyone introducing themselves properly. *It's a bit like the television being on*, she thinks, *except these are real people, and the drama is playing out right here in Westminster Crescent.*

After undoing the gown, Helen slips out of her nightie, reaching around to the dull pain she suspects is arthritis. She rubs the area then stops moving. Waits for it to pass, hoping it's nothing more than the result of sleeping several hours longer than usual.

Pulling a brush through her hair, Helen simply cannot believe there are four people downstairs—five if you include Sipsworth.

Laughter floats up the stairs as Dr. Jamal and Cecil tell some kind of story.

What's she going to do with them all? At least for now they seem to be entertaining each other.

When Helen enters the sitting room, Dr. Jamal and Cecil are on their knees examining the oxygen chamber.

Both men stand when they notice her watching them. "You look a picture," Cecil says. "What a lovely blouse . . . bluebells, if I'm not mistaken."

The librarian points at Helen with her walking stick. "Only three months more and they'll be popping up on the riverbanks."

Cecil laughs deeply. "Snowdrops first, mind you."

Half the food laid out from the night before has already been eaten. Dr. Jamal swallows what's in his mouth. "They're actually toxic if ingested, snowdrops."

Cecil's eyes grow. "Are they indeed?"

"Yes, we had a child brought in last year . . . a little girl."

The librarian makes a pained face and looks at her son, who is sitting on the carpet watching the mouse. "Oh, I hope she was okay in the end."

"She was fine, but it gave her parents a scare. I believe it's the alkaloid compounds . . . they're in daffodils, too."

Cecil wags his finger in the air. "Oh, oh, this is very good to know, I'll warn any of my customers that have toddlers and dogs."

Helen approaches the group and looks at everyone. "Who would like some tea?"

Fortunately, just three hands go up, as after asking Helen realises she only has three mugs—and one has a chip in the rim.

Dominic is still watching Sipsworth intently and not listening to anything being said.

"He likes sweet drinks," the librarian informs Helen, "even though they're very bad for his teeth."

In the kitchen Helen finds the box of tea bags. Fills the kettle. Leans on the counter. Stares at the toaster. The conversation in the other room seems bottomless. How perfect strangers have so much to talk about, Helen can't understand.

When the tea is ready, she carries it in on a tray. Sets a sugar bowl on the table. Returns to the kitchen. Pours two glasses of lemonade, one for herself and one for Dominic.

Even with drinks in their hands, her guests continue the chatter. Sipsworth is on his wheel, contributing to the conversation with a continuous rattle.

How impossible it's going to be to get rid of everyone, Helen thinks. All she wants now is to enjoy her Sunday in peace. Still, without the people in this room her mouse might not be alive. The realisation of this forces a reluctant smile.

"Why don't we go into the back garden?" she announces.

Cecil puts down his empty cup with the chip. "If only I'd known, I could have brought a barbecue set!"

When they are outside, the moss-coated patio stones and overgrown bushes nudge the conversation in a new direction. Cecil points out the weeds from the shrubs. Goes over his plans for when things warm up a bit.

Dr. Jamal asks where the security light is going, and Cecil scans the back wall of Helen's home with both hands like a medium, explaining the procedure for drilling into brick.

Helen is standing at a distance from everyone until Dominic appears at her side.

"Does . . . er . . . your mouse's water have to be a certain temperature?"

Helen thinks for a moment. "There wasn't anything in the book about that, so I think room temperature is fine."

"They must drink it cold in winter."

"Yes, Dominic, I imagine they do." Helen is surprised by how different he seems now that he's comfortable with her. She wonders if there's a specific name for his condition, and if treatment is pharmacological, psychotherapeutic, or a combination of the two.

He seems interested then in something at the far end of Helen's garden, beyond the hedgerow, a shallow sleeve of woods that divides Westminster Crescent from farm fields. "If I was a mouse, I'd live out there."

Helen follows his gaze.

"But it's a long way for them," Dominic goes on. "Because mice are smaller."

"I once lived far away, Dominic."

He must have sensed the change in Helen's tone because he turns to look at her.

"In Australia," she goes on.

"Did you have mice there?"

Helen smiles. "Since you ask, I had two. One big and one little."

When Cecil strides over holding the stem of some plant to show Helen, Dominic scoots off to join his mother.

"I need to talk to you about this perennial, missus . . . but first, I think the boy's mother would like to sit down. Is there a chair I could get for her?"

Helen leads Cecil inside. "In the bedroom. There's one by the bed."

"Right-o, then."

She listens to the shopkeeper's boots clomp up the stairs, then thump across the landing into her bedroom.

In his tank, Sipsworth is moving bits of tissue around, as if getting ready for bed.

Cecil passes by a moment later holding the chair, which looks oddly small in his arms.

"Did you know you've got a loose floorboard on the stairs?"

Helen goes to speak but Cecil holds up one hand. "I'll put it on my list."

Outside, Dr. Jamal is deep in conversation with the librarian and her son. When he sees Helen, he wipes some crumbs from his mouth. "Dominic wanted me to ask how Sipsworth is doing."

"Very well. He's like a new mouse this morning. I'll go and get him if he's not already asleep."

Back inside, Helen feels breathless—which is not unexpected, she supposes. It *is* the afternoon and she's only had a glass of lemonade.

Sipsworth is on his castle, signalling with both paws.

"You're supposed to be in bed, young man."

He pops onto the slipper, but as Helen steps out through the French door, the noise and weak sunshine sweep him into the toe.

Dr. Jamal strides over. "So glad he's doing well."

Helen stares at the slipper in her hand. "It was last night, I believe, that he turned a corner. I'm sure of it."

Dr. Jamal looks past Helen into the house. Raises an eyebrow. "I think there's someone knocking. More visitors?"

The librarian and her son are over by some shrubs with Cecil, so Helen sets the slipper down in the empty chair.

Opening the mustard door with the noisy letterbox, Helen finds a middle-aged man in brown corduroy trousers and a navy jumper.

"Hello," he says. "I'm Dave Richards, from number twenty-three. I just wanted to see if everything was all right."

Helen doesn't know what to say. There's something familiar about the man she can't put her finger on.

"It's just that we had a leak last month," he goes on. "And it took men from the water board two days to work out it was coming from an old overflow pipe running under the house from when there were factories in the area. My wife saw the cars and white van out front and wondered if you might be having the same problem."

"Oh, no, there's nothing like that here. Just a few friends over is all."

"Oh, good. Well, sorry to trouble you then."

As he turns to go, Helen remembers something from the shape of his body.

"Excuse me, Mr. Richards . . ."

The man turns.

"Did you by any chance leave a fish tank out for rubbish collection recently?"

The neighbour frowns. "How did you know that?"

"I saw it," Helen replies quickly. "Sitting out on the pavement."

"I didn't leave it in your way, did I? To be honest I was half asleep."

"Oh no. It's just that . . ."

"I was clearing out the shed because my daughter has gotten into carpentry of all things, and my wife thought the shed would be a nice workshop for her."

Helen thinks quickly. "No more fish then?"

The man chuckles. "We never had fish to begin with. When my daughter was nine, she had a gerbil . . . what did she call it . . . Freckles!"

"A gerbil?"

"Yes, lovely little creature . . . don't live long though. She was so attached to the thing it seemed ruthless to just toss its home away with all the creature's gubbins, so I put it in the shed."

"I see," Helen says.

"She's seventeen now."

"Who is?" Helen asks.

"Our daughter, Zaara. She's in college but wants to drop out and do woodworking, so my wife and I thought she could do it in the shed . . . just to make sure it's what she really wants and not just a phase."

Helen smiles sadly. "Everything's a phase, Mr. Richards."

He nods politely. "Yes, well, I'll let you get back to your guests then."

"Thank you," Helen says, "for thinking to come over and warn me about the leak."

"My pleasure, and if you need anything, we're at number twenty-three. The one with the white Volkswagen."

Helen closes the door.

As she turns around Dr. Jamal is rushing toward her.

"He's gone, Helen."

She feels hot and shaky and sick.

"Who's gone?"

But she knows.

As Dr. Jamal leads her to the back garden, Helen can hear Dominic calling the name she had given him. Her hands are trembling, but she lifts the slipper and looks inside. Tilts it. Apart from two tiny rolls of poo, it's completely empty.

In a loud voice, Cecil warns everyone not to take a step without first looking. The shopkeeper is on his hands and knees sifting leaves and sticks. The librarian is parting the bare hedgerow with her walking cane.

The pain in Helen's back returns with great force and she feels unsteady. But Dr. Jamal is there and guides her into the chair. Her throat is tight. It's a struggle to breathe. Helen blinks furiously to clear her vision, but everything is blurred as if coming undone.

MONDAY

TUESDAY

35.

WHEN HELEN OPENS her eyes, she is lying in a bed with an IV in her arm.

She knows she is in hospital from the familiar sounds of machines.

But there is no one around she can call out to and ask what on earth has happened.

Her throat is so dry it's like broken glass—but then her eyes are closing again. Helen feels there is something urgent she needs to do—but cannot muster the strength to stay afloat.

WEDNESDAY

THURSDAY

36.

WHEN HELEN WAKES again her room is filled with soft, white light. There's a nurse doing something with her arm.

"Hello there, Dr. Cartwright, it's Kathy. Do you remember me?"

Helen nods weakly.

"Don't try and talk. Just rest. Dr. Jamal will be in this afternoon, but I'll call to let him know you're properly awake."

"Nurse . . ."

"You've had a cardiac intervention, Dr. Cartwright . . . very minimal, but it's important you rest. In a few hours you'll feel yourself again, I promise." Kathy bends down and holds both of Helen's hands in hers. "Dr. Jamal had you in surgery within sixty minutes . . . I think that's a record."

"Where am I?"

"You're in Meadowpark Hospital, Dr. Cartwright."

Helen nods because she understands the words and recognizes the name but can't seem to put them in context.

"There's someone here to see you. He's been waiting a long time. I'll send him in."

A moment after the nurse leaves, a large, disheveled-looking man enters her room. He's got a bunch of grapes in one hand and a bunch of flowers in the other.

"Hello, missus."

It's the voice Helen recognizes first. "Cecil?"

"The one and only. You gave us quite a scare on Sunday."

Then Helen remembers. The truth of what's happened pours in. She has the slipper in her hand. But there's nothing. No one. It's empty.

"Sipsworth!" She gasps.

Cecil pats her shoulder.

"Be calm now, Helen. Please don't be worrying yourself."

"Where is he? Did you find him?"

"Now then, Helen. I want you to relax because he's okay, he's quite happy . . . I'm sure of it."

"Did you find him, Cecil? Where's my mouse?"

"After you left in an ambulance with Dr. Jamal, Dominic and I stayed behind and searched every inch of the garden and when it got dark, we left food and shelter in case he decided to come back."

Helen feels the disappointment as if it were something physical, something inside of her body that has finally broken and will never work again.

"Before you jump to conclusions now, missus, about him being lost an' all, remember that he left the slipper of his own accord, which tells you that he had important mouse business to take care of. He's an animal . . . and they're made for living outside . . . truth be told, the outside is more their world than the one you made for him at Westminster Crescent, as lovely as it was."

"But . . ." Helen protests.

"The way I see it, you nursed him back to full strength so that he could continue on his way."

Helen takes a deep breath, realising that while she lies here, her mouse is out there somewhere, doing and seeing things she can't even imagine.

"But he's such a small thing . . ." she pleads. "And so good-natured. What if something . . ."

"A clever mouse like that will find no harm. I installed the outside security light and have been going back every morning and night to have a look. It seems our friend has returned to the world of mice."

Cecil is doing his best, but his words are like birds with nowhere to land.

Helen imagines Sipsworth's small body.

There he is now. Foraging in leaves. Dangling from hedgerow branches on the quest for a berry. His eyes are bright, and his coat ruffled with tiny stars of frost.

The way he would use his tail to help balance, she will always remember.

Cecil takes a paisley handkerchief from his pocket. Gives it to Helen.

"Stop worrying, missus. He's out there doing what every mouse is supposed to be doing, because of you."

Helen lifts her head from the pillow. "No, Cecil . . . because of *us*."

When Dr. Jamal arrives a few hours later, Helen is listening to the nurses talk excitedly in the hallway about all the Christmas decorations going up. Cecil has gone back to the shop, and is no doubt working to fulfill the orders for tree stands and tinsel that were called in by telephone during his absence.

When Dr. Jamal takes a seat at her bedside, Helen sits up. She is fully awake now and has even been walking to the toilet.

"What happened to me?"

"Nothing too major . . . a standard non-ST-elevation myocardial infarction. But if we hadn't been there . . ."

Helen understands. "A partial occlusion, was it?"

"Exactly. But your vessel became fully patent after a PCI . . . which would have been called a PTCA when you were practising, no stents then. How are you feeling? Any pain at all?"

"Oh, I'm fine, thanks to you. But Sipsworth . . ."

Dr. Jamal shuffles in his seat. Looks at the grapes on Helen's bedside table. "I've been thinking about him, too. I went back after surgery to have a look. Cecil had keys made. I hope you don't mind."

As evening washes through her room, Nurse Kathy appears.

"I'm here to help you dress, Dr. Cartwright. Our second-favourite cardiologist is going to drive you home. He's just finishing some paperwork."

When her clothes have been put on, Helen sits in the chair. She is alone again because Kathy has gone to get her bag of what she suspects is the standard post-infarction medical treatment—a big bag of pills.

When the door opens it's Dr. Jamal with a wheelchair.

"Hospital policy, I'm afraid."

In the lift, Dr. Jamal asks Helen if Cecil should pop over with some dinner.

Helen shakes her head. "Sleep is all I need now," she says quietly.

× × ×

In the car, Helen doesn't recognise much of the place where she grew up. The town has been decorated for Christmas, but the coloured bulbs and glittering banners seem false and clownish. A light snow is dusting the lanes and the roads and the many small gardens.

When they pull up outside her house on Westminster Crescent, the snow is really coming down, thick and slow like clumps of fur ripped from winter's back. Dr. Jamal comes around to her door. It's colder than she imagined, and Helen can feel the hands of winter burrowing into her clothes.

"Easy does it, Helen . . . the path is very slippery . . ."

When they get in through the mustard door, the house feels empty, as though drained of any life in the days she has been away. Dr. Jamal puts on the kitchen light and asks her again if she isn't hungry. He could heat up some beans or open a can of soup.

"I'm putting your pills on the counter. Unless you want me to take them upstairs?"

Helen is in the sitting room, trying not to look down at the empty fish tank. "Kitchen's fine, thank you."

When Dr. Jamal appears again, he asks if she wants the lamp or the telly on. Helen shakes her head without explaining why.

For a while he just stands there.

"I'll be fine now, Dr. Jamal. You can go home. Just be careful driving."

"It feels a bit weird leaving you here."

Helen turns to face him. "I wouldn't be here at all if it wasn't for you."

"You have my mobile number?"

"Stop worrying. I just need a few moments to adjust."

Helen knows why Dr. Jamal is lingering, but she can't bring herself to say his name out loud. Not yet.

It'll take some time.

For a long while after he's driven off, she just sits there.

FRIDAY

37.

IT IS PAST midnight when Helen decides to make the long journey upstairs to bed. All the major news programmes have been over for hours. And the bright pubs of the town—each dressed for Christmas in its own way—will be shutting their doors, as the streets fill with knots of people, traipsing home in clouds of breathless excitement.

From somewhere in the house, Helen discerns a light tapping. Cecil must have adjusted the heat, on account of the weather.

It's a struggle to stand, but once she's up, Helen moves lugubriously through the dark sitting room toward the kitchen. Passing the French door, garish light suddenly floods the patio.

Helen stops. Sighs. Shakes her head.

If Cecil spent as much time looking after himself as he did worrying about break-ins, they'd all be better off.

Part of her wants to linger there, just in case, but she knows it would not be the wisest thing.

The empty patio seems strange in the shock of bright yellow. But in time Helen supposes it's something she'll get used to as nothing more than a stage for memory to play out its fancies.

She waits beside the French door for the security light to click off.

Remembers the night she brought him inside.

The soiled box where he'd been sleeping.

The cold dripping rain and that business with the cat.

Then both slippers stuck fast in glue. Oh, the rage she had felt, which wasn't rage at all, but a condition of loneliness.

Helen peers down at the place where she caught herself. But instead of two plastic traps, conjured by memory to fill the darkness ahead, her eye is drawn to something outside, pressing against the French door, a small figure, a smudge against the falling snow, but plump and grey, with one paw on the glass.

ACKNOWLEDGMENTS

The author wishes to express his gratitude to everyone at Godine, without whom there would be nothing in your hands at this moment. That team includes Tammy Ackerman, interior design; David Allender, publisher; Beth Blachman, copyeditor; Virginia Downes, production; Dylan Gray, logistics; Celia Johnson, editor; Linda Johnson, customer service; Leisa Perrotta, accounting; Doris Troy, proofreader; and, most of all, my beloved editor and friend, Joshua Bodwell, who never tired of discussing that most noble creature, *Mus musculus* over tea and Bakewell tarts.

For the outstanding cover art, special thanks to James Weston Lewis.

The author is also grateful for the hard work of Susanna Lea and her team, Thérèse Coen, Mark Kessler, Una McKeown, Stephen M. Morrison, and Lauren Wendelken.

Special praise must also be extended to my wife, Christina Daigneault, and daughter, Madeleine Van Booy, Long Island Bird & Exotics Veterinary Clinic, along with Bernie Monteleone MD, and Captain Kathleen Sexton for advice and mentorship, respectively.

This book was completed in Room 26 at the Royal Society of Medicine in London, where the kind and patient staff kept me in tea, biscuits, and instant hot chocolate.

Unfortunately, I did not see any mice during my stay.

BOOK CLUB DISCUSSION GUIDE

1. This novel is set in the town where the author grew up, but hasn't lived in for thirty years. Why do you think he chose to do that? If you wrote a book, where would you set it?
2. What do you think Helen means when she says: "And herein lies the cruel paradox of human existence—not that you die, but that all happiness eventually turns against you."
3. Helen has returned to the town of her childhood after living abroad for sixty years. If you no longer live where you were brought up, would you ever consider moving back to where you grew up in your eighties, like Helen?
4. The book is set in the present tense, as opposed to the past tense, which most authors use. How do you think this changes the experience for the reader?
5. Why do you think Helen is just "waiting to die"? Can you empathize with her state of mind? Why do you think she is not interested in forming relationships with people in the town? What would you do for someone who felt this way?

6. Helen goes from being irritated by the mouse to making the animal little meals and explaining the plots of films on television. In your opinion, what causes this change in her? Has anything similar ever happened to you, where you did a complete 180 in your opinion of something or someone?
7. "The only consolation of being the last to go," Helen admits, "is knowing the people you loved the most won't suffer the way you do in their absence." Do you agree with this line?
8. "The only real proof of her advanced age is a chronic, persistent feeling of defeat, aching limbs, and the power of invisibility to anyone between the ages of ten and fifty." Why do you think this is one of the most underlined sentences by readers in the entire novel?
9. The novel takes place over a few weeks. During that time, Helen's life changed dramatically. Has there ever been a short period in your life where things changed as quickly?
10. One of the main characters in this novel is a creature that many people are afraid of or disgusted by. Do you think this story will change how people view rodents?
11. In some ways, the reader sees Helen as simply an elderly woman until the middle of the book, where there's a big surprise for the reader. Do you think this moment in the novel will affect how you view older people from now on?
12. Near the end of the book, there are some blank pages after the usual day setting. Why do you think the author did this?

13. For two years, the author looked after two mice he rescued from feeder tanks at pet shops. Do you think this experience was vital to the novel?
14. The author is also an EMT crew chief working in New York City and, during college, volunteered briefly in a nursing home. Do you think these experiences might have influenced the novel?
15. In this novel, Helen is saved twice by an animal. When she falls down the well as a girl, it's a dog; then seventy-five years later, it's a mouse. Do you believe animals have the power to heal us?
16. After being alone for so many years, most of Helen's initial interactions with people are to ask them for things. Why do you think they respond favorably and go out of their way to help? Do you think most people are like this? Are you like this?

A REAL MOUSE?

FROM 2020 TO 2022, the author and his wife cared for two mice. The first, Tiresias, only lived six months and required round-the-clock health care, as he was afflicted with a congenital disease like COPD in humans. When Simon had to travel from New York to California during the COVID pandemic, mice were not allowed on commercial flights (they still aren't), so he was forced to drive across the country to continue palliative care for his mouse.

Whilst in Santa Barbara for two months with Tiresias, Simon wrote another novel, *The Presence of Absence*, which is a meditation on life, death, love, and memory.

Tiresias passed away on the drive back to New York, on the twentieth floor of a casino hotel Simon had smuggled him into.

Devastated, but not wanting a "rebound mouse," the author waited two months before stepping back inside the pet shop, where he had rescued Tiresias from one of the "feeder tanks" where mice are bred and sold to snake owners: a practice the author finds abhorrent, believing that at least in nature the mouse has a chance to escape.

As living a mouse-less life was just not an option, he and his wife looked over the many small rodents playing, drinking, and sleeping in one of the big pet shop enclosures. Then, in a strange gesture, one of the mice walked calmly over to the glass and put its paw up. The electricity was unmistakable, as the author and the mouse stared at one another. Then he scampered away on all fours (the mouse, not the author) to the water bottle, and the author's wife pointed out that they [his tank mates] wouldn't even let him get a "sip's worth.'"

And that's how he got his name.

Sipsworth lived for two years (a long time for a mouse!), giving and receiving love and affection every precious day.

"The mouse with the Mona Lisa smile . . ."

THE AUTHOR'S GUIDE TO THE PERFECT CUP OF TEA

1. I would suggest British or Irish black tea, such as PG Tips, Typhoo Tea, Yorkshire Tea, or Barry's Tea. You can buy it in bags or loose. If you have a pot and a strainer, loose tea will give you a richer cup. By the way, the reason you'll almost never have a "proper" cup of tea in a restaurant outside of the UK and Ireland is that hot water almost always comes from a coffee machine, rather than from a kettle, which, quite literally, boils the bejesus out of it.
2. Warm the cup, mug, or pot by swishing around some hot water (bone china is preferred as it holds heat longer), then pour it out. Pour freshly boiling water onto the tea bag, which should be in the cup by now; otherwise, you're going to need a cloth.
3. Cover with a small dish (retain that heat! Nobody likes warm tea). I always steep for four minutes, as after that the taste can be quite bitter. The caffeine is released first, so the length of steeping really comes down to a preference for flavor.
4. Remove the tea bag and discard. Though some people (like my wife) use tea bags twice. She does this

because reusing them reminds her of her grandmother, who grew up during the Depression.

5. I'd say ninety percent of British and Irish people add milk, with about fifty percent adding sugar. In the British Army, a "brew" is tea with full-fat milk and two sugars. I like to use lactose-free, semi-skimmed (or two percent in the US) milk, and when I'm feeling naughty, three glorious heaped teaspoons of sugar.
6. To get the most pleasure out of your "tea break," turn off your phone and do nothing but sip and reflect on the day so far. Many people like to brew tea and then talk. In most British and Irish households, if there's a crisis, the first step to resolving it is to put the kettle on.
7. Now, accompanying snacks . . . well, it's completely up to you. If you're of the old school, then a slice of fruitcake might be in order. Most octogenarians I visit in the UK and Ireland keep a tin on hand. The cake might be harder than calculus, but that's what the tea is for. My grandmother, being from Jamaica, liked bulla cake or ginger cake. Scottish people take shortbread. The Irish may enjoy some heavily buttered soda bread. Yum! Some people like biscuits, which Americans call cookies. However, British and Irish biscuits are a little less sweet and more brittle than their transatlantic brethren. My favorites (and Helen's too) include Custard Creams, Malted Milk, and perhaps the reigning monarch of all biscuits, the humble but ubiquitous Digestive.

8. If you're a real tea-lover, then perhaps, like me, you'll build your perfect tea set. If you want a picture, just DM me on Instagram. Every item on the tray has a story behind it that's meaningful to me. Every afternoon at 1600, I carry the tray from my study to the kitchen, where I brew a pot of Yorkshire Tea. For guests, I sometimes blend a second pot with Fortnum & Mason's Fortmason blend.

A NOTE ABOUT THE AUTHOR

Simon Van Booy is the prize-winning, bestselling author of 15 books for adults and children, including *The Illusion of Separateness*, and *The Presence of Absence*. He is the anthologist of three volumes of philosophy, and has written for the *New York Times*, the *Financial Times*, the *Washington Post*, NPR, and the BBC.

His books have been translated into many languages and optioned for film and television. Raised in rural North Wales, Simon currently lives in New York, where he is also a private book editor.

In his spare time, Simon is an EMT crew chief and Lieutenant of [medical] Training for Gotham Volunteer EMS. His other joys include spending time with his wife and daughter, model trains, longcase clocks, and the operas of Handel.

A NOTE ON THE TYPE

Sipsworth has been set in Caslon. This modern version is based on the early-eighteenth-century roman designs of British printer William Caslon I, whose typefaces were so popular that they were employed for the first setting of the Declaration of Independence in 1776. Eric Gill's humanist typeface Gill Sans, from 1928, has been used for display.

Book Design & Composition by Tammy Ackerman